A little
grown-up for you
at almost 6 but I know
you can keep it until
you are almost 99. And confi-
dent that before then you will
read it to many children & grand-
son of your own.
Love
Nana & Papa
1991

MARK
MAKES HIS
MOVE

MARK
MAKES HIS
MOVE

MARIAN POTTER

WILLIAM MORROW & COMPANY, INC.
NEW YORK

Printed in the United States of America.
1 2 3 4 5 6 7 8 9 10
Library of Congress Cataloging-in-Publication Data
Potter, Marian.
Mark makes his move.
Summary: Eleven-year-old Mark tries to find a
solution to two of his most pressing problems: how
to stop the Skinner brothers from bullying him and how
to save his friend's, old Mrs. McSwiggen's, property
from land developers.
[1. Bullies—Fiction. 2. Friendship—Fiction.
3. Family life—Fiction] I. Title.
PZ7.P853Mar 1986   [Fic]   86-8357
ISBN 0-688-06220-2

For Carrie, Susie, Becca, and Nick

MARK
MAKES HIS
MOVE

CHAPTER ONE

A litter of beer cans and the battered school bus shelter were the only signs of humanity along the dismal stretch of road. Mark Frye had named the forsaken tract overgrown with swamp alders the Wilderness Area after a special program he'd seen on public television. The three kids who had lived down the road had moved to the Sunbelt. Now only Mark and the Skinner boys were picked up at the Wilderness Area stop. Today, especially since he was carrying cash, he felt edgy.

Mark jumped when his dog, Ozro, bounded out of the brush. "Hey, we had a deal. If I didn't put you in the dog run, you wouldn't follow me." He tried to keep Ozro's big, muddy feet off his warm-up jacket and the dog's slobbers off his face. Then Mark realized that Ozro might be some protection. He had never attacked anything but a groundhog, but the Skinners didn't know that. "All right. You can stay until the bus comes. Then go home when I say to."

Mark sank his fingers into the soft fur around Ozro's ears. Mark's mother called Ozro a big yellow mutt, but he wasn't dandelion yellow. Now that would be some dog. Mark thought of Ozro as a big towheaded dog. His hair was nearly the color of Mark's, and Mom called him a towhead. Their ears were different. Ozro's were soft and neat against his head and stood out only when he needed them. Mark's ears stood out all the time. Mom made him keep his hair long enough to brush down over his ears, so the light wouldn't shine through them.

Ozro pulled away to sniff around the bus shelter. A pile of rabbit droppings sent him into a frenzy of barking, and he was off on the trail of a rabbit, ignoring Mark's commands to stay. Now Mark was on his own.

He considered gathering a pile of stones to threaten La Vern and Jack Skinner, but they'd know he was bluffing. The Skinners were able to smell fear the way a mean dog could. Mark pulled up the hood of his jacket and thrust his hands into the front pouch pocket. He hoped he looked big and tough in the heavy sweatshirt his older brother, Scott, had outgrown. Since he couldn't make his small blue eyes dark and fierce, he squinted to make them even smaller for a shrewd, steely look.

As he did each morning when the Skinners weren't around, he walked as tall as he could under a board that stuck out at one corner of the crudely built bus shelter. When he had started fifth grade last September, that board had cleared his head by half an inch. He was eleven now and could still walk under it, but he hoped for the day he'd have to duck. His dad had assured him it would come. He'd take off on a growing streak, shoot up all at once, just as Scott and Dad himself had done.

Mark thought of Dad driving alone on the highway and wished he were with him. Still, Dad had a big rig and a CB radio that must be a lot of company.

Mark felt like the Indian in the painting, *The End of the Trail*, which hung in his room at Hardin Township Elementary. He crouched over, imitating the Indian's defeated attitude. The Indian had a horse, which was more than Mark had.

Still crouched, he was an easy target for the Skinners, who rose from a clump of alders like defensive linebackers set to sack the quarterback. Jack pushed him forward, flat on his face. La Vern jumped on him and held him down. He could feel their hands going through his pockets. La Vern was heavier, but Jack was quicker. They both smelled like moist, stale soda crackers.

"What's the matter? Are you ticklish?" La Vern shrieked.

"Give him the salt shaker!" Jack yelled in glee.

They pulled him to his feet and shook him violently. The Skinners knew it was the last day to bring money for those book-club paperbacks. They were trying to shake coins out of him as if he were a piggy bank. If that didn't work, the next move would be to break the bank.

The blur of the yellow bus coming around the curve was as welcome to Mark as a ship on the horizon to a marooned sailor. La Vern and Jack yanked his jacket down to his knees, gave him a final shake, and shoved ahead of him onto the bus. He pulled up his jacket, tucked in his shirt, and felt inside his belt to make sure the three quarters fastened with masking tape were still there. He had lived through the worst part of another day.

The next morning was promising. Mark waited on the front porch hoping to get a ride to school with his family. His big sister, Kelli, waited in their old Chrysler in the driveway.

She gave the car a few test roars of power and then tilted her head to listen to the motor idle. The pale March sun shone on her blond hair. Kelli was pretty even when her long hair was peeled back and pinned up the way it had to be when she worked at Charley's Chicken. There she had to wear a little red hat that looked like a chicken's comb.

Mark could hear Mom's high heels pounding about inside. Her friends said Linda Frye sure managed to get a lot of things done. Mark thought she hurried too much and didn't listen enough.

Mom's heels hammered across the porch. "Let's see

now. I've put in a load of wash. Have meat out to thaw, called the YWCA." She seemed to be talking more to herself than to Mark. She stopped to smooth her collar and straighten her skirt. "I hope I'm all put together." She pushed at her new curly permanent. She was really a neat-looking mom, although she claimed her eyebrows were too heavy and her jaw too square. Mark knew she was always pleased when people couldn't believe eighteen-year-old Kelli was her daughter.

She rummaged in her big purse as she clicked down the steps. Hurrying to the car, she looked up and called, "Scott, get down out of that tree. Come on. Kelli's wasting gas."

Scott dropped down like a rock in front of Mom. As she staggered back over a hole in the ground, her purse went flying, and she caught her heel under an exposed tree root.

"Sorry," Scott mumbled. "You said come down." He stuck his hands in his jacket pockets, hunched his shoulders, and went to the car.

Mom loosened her heel and picked up her purse. "I'm telling you for the last time, Mark, stop digging in this yard. You and that big yellow mutt."

Mom frequently passed right over Mark except to give some silly order. He had stopped construction on his interstate highway under the pine tree a year ago. Ozro hadn't dug there since he was a pup. Mark followed Mom to the car, hoping to point out these things.

The door of the car shuddered as Mom got in and closed it. The window would roll down only halfway, but enough for Mom to give Mark orders. "Get a shovel out of the garage, and fill up all those holes."

"Instead of going to school?" Mark asked hopefully.

"Of course not. Now run on down to the bus stop." Mom made it sound like some kind of lark.

"Mom, make Kelli drive me to school."

"No way." Kelli was emphatic. "It's out of our way. I'm already late for work. I'd have to turn around, and I'm having trouble getting this rust bucket into reverse."

Mark patted Mom's frizzy hair. "Let me go to the doctor with you. See how Scott's back is doing."

Mom shook her head. "Why don't you wear your good school jacket? That thing hangs down over the seat of your pants."

"Listen, Mom, let me go with you."

Mom sighed. "Now, Mark, we've all got a job to do. Dad's out on the interstates fighting for his life driving a truck. Kelli's due at Charley's Chicken. Scott has to see the doctor. I have my Y course. Remember your swimming class after school today. Now put Ozro in his run and go to school. That's your job."

As Mark watched the car turn into Hardin Road, he wondered how Mom kept the whole family programmed without a computer. At the end of the driveway he gave their mailbox on its leaning post a whack to hear its hollow ring. "Frye" it proclaimed in the fancy script Mom had learned to write at a YWCA course. "Wheeler," "Linda," "Kelli," "Scott" were evenly spaced beneath. Mark's name was squeezed in at the bottom as if he hadn't been on Mom's schedule.

He was glad he hadn't been named after Dad. Some people thought Wheeler was Dad's nickname because he drove a truck. They didn't know that it was an old family name.

Cautiously Mark passed the rutted dirt lane that led to the house where the Skinners lived on Hardin Creek. There was no sign of La Vern and Jack, which meant they were already waiting in ambush at the Wilderness Area. Many mornings he had begun to feel relieved by the thought that the Skinners were home with bellyaches when they jumped yelling out of nowhere to push him around.

Having a brother thirteen years old was no help at the bus stop. The bus to Scott's junior high came earlier, so he was always gone when the Skinners bullied Mark. Scott wouldn't be much concerned anyhow. Mark recalled how his tall brother had walked to the car that morning and imitated Scott's slump as he plodded along. Lately Scott always seemed hunched over, walking away from him.

Mark had considered telling Mom that the Skinners picked on him. But the phrase made him think of a pitiful, bloody chick pecked by the other chickens. If he could get Mom to listen, she'd probably say everyone had a job to do. His was to beat up on the Skinner boys.

Mornings when Mark tried to hide in the underbrush until the bus appeared, the Skinners, like a pack of hounds, had tracked him in the snow and knocked him into the swamp ice. He might be more successful in hiding now that most of the snow was gone.

That morning the WHGR radio announcer had said they'd reached March 21, the vernal equinox, when the lengths of the day and of the night were equal. He kicked at the dirty snow on the north side of the bus shelter and wondered if the vernal equinox was a new school holiday he hadn't heard of. Maybe the bus wasn't coming. Could be school was closed because all the snow days hadn't been used. Still, the radio hadn't mentioned any such luck.

A rustling sound alerted him, and he was relieved to see a robin pecking among soggy fallen leaves. Then Mark heard a car approaching and recognized Mrs. McSwiggen, his neighbor, in her station wagon.

She saw his signal and pulled off the road opposite the shelter. "What is it, Mark? I'm in a hurry to get in line for a household sale that opens at nine o'clock. Then I'm going to an auction at ten."

Mark crossed the road so she wouldn't need to shout. Mrs. McSwiggen was wearing her bubble-style wig, which she usually wore only on weekends.

"You've got a bug or something on your glasses."

"You need specks yourself, Mark. Those are my initials, E. F. M., Edna Florence McSwiggen. That's the latest." She turned her head to look in her rearview mirror. Her nose was sharp enough, but her cheek and neck were blurred in a sag of wrinkles.

"Guess what? I saw a robin," Mark announced.

"Saw three a week ago. Now I must get a payday move on, Mark." She gripped the steering wheel.

"I was just wondering . . ." Mark tried to think of something to detain her until the bus came. The Skinners were due any minute. "Oh, yes, I clipped a bunch of coupons for you out of Sunday's paper and some magazines. Do you think you'd ever use Triple Twist pretzels?"

"Bring the coupons over after school. I'll take a look. There might be a coupon war coming on."

Mark hooked his arms over the car window. "You know that family that moved to the Sunbelt? Well, sometimes I think of the Sunbelt as a big round ball with this huge flashing belt."

"Never struck me that way." She accelerated the motor.

"Do you know anybody with a bunch of nice kids who might want to move into the next house?" Mark pointed down the road. Before she could answer, he had another thought. "Say, Mrs. McSwiggen, where is the household sale?"

"Out on Route Forty-eight." She gently moved his arms from her car window.

"You go right by Hardin Township Elementary to get there." Mark opened the car door just as the Skinners came in sight.

"All right. Hop in. I'll answer questions on the way."

Mark settled into the front seat. It was mighty handy to have a neighbor like Mrs. McSwiggen.

CHAPTER TWO

Jack Skinner's dark, glowering looks from across the classroom throughout the day made Mark dread the next one. He tried to get his mind on something else and selected the new issue of *My Weekly Reader* for sustained reading, which was the last period. A diagram on the first page set him off on sustained thinking. It showed ancient tribesmen in an arid land climbing down a long ladder to an underground river, their only water supply.

The picture made him think of the Zanzutu tribe, which he had made up after watching a *National Geographic* television special. The tribe he imagined had some of the actual customs he'd seen, and he'd added traits of other primitive people he'd read about. He also found it convenient to invent a few practices for them.

He looked at the date on the school newspaper and

decided the Zanzutus would know about the vernal equinox. They'd have rocks piled up so the sun shone right through a certain notch at noon. The Zanzutus could be and do whatever he liked. They were his; Mark had created them.

He studied the long ladder in the drawing. That's how his Zanzutus had escaped. They had been underground getting water when two atomic bombs were exchanged. Mark himself had been blown into a cave formed by the underground river that eventually brought him to the Zanzutus.

He, Mark Frye, and the primitive Zanzutus were the only human beings left on earth. If they and their children were to know anything about modern science and technology, he'd have to teach them. This was an awful responsibility. He felt woefully inadequate for the job. Here he was, a kid of the twentieth century from an advanced country who wasn't even sure how a telescope worked. He knew more about potato chips than about computer chips. He didn't understand how sounds, let alone pictures, could come through the air without wires.

He'd once done a neat science experiment of iron filings forming a pattern around a magnet, but electricity was still a greater mystery to him than it had been to Ben Franklin. He gave up his first idea of building the Zanzutus an electric water pump. He'd better go farther back in history. By the time school was dismissed, he was wondering how wood was curved to form a wheel. Clay jars fastened to a rope of jungle vines passing over a wheel would help the Zanzutus draw water. Mark had seen such a wheel once over a fake well where people threw pennies and made wishes.

As Mark wormed his way through the crowd to the bus, he had a nagging feeling that he was forgetting something, but he tried to put the thought out of his mind. The midafternoon traffic was light, so the driver let Mark off right at his door.

Ozro, loping on a slant, came to meet him. The dog's winter coat shed as Mark petted him. "Safe for another day, Ozro. The township police didn't get you, and the Skinners didn't get me."

Mark jumped over the excavations of his interstate. "Mom!" he called as he went in the side door to the kitchen.

"She's at cake decorating class." Kelli's voice came from her room down the hall.

Mark took a raw hot dog from the refrigerator. He wondered about Mom's class. Were there speed drills to see who could decorate the fastest? His mouth watered as he thought of the sweet mess. Maybe neatness counted. Could Mom write "Happy Birthday" in her fancy script with a stream of soft sugar icing? Suppose she flunked rose buds on the final exam?

Kelli came to the kitchen with a note in her hand. It fluttered when she sneezed twice. With reddened eyes and runny nose she didn't look as pretty as usual, even with her shining, long hair framing her face.

"Darn allergy," she said, taking a tissue from a box on the kitchen counter.

"Got any clues yet?" Mark asked.

"Not for sure. But keep Ozro out of this house, Mark. It could be dog hair, dust, tree blooms, fibers, almost anything or a lot of things, the doctor said. He wants me to take a bunch of tests."

She looked at the note and proclaimed in an official voice, "Orders from Mom. Now hear this: 'Scott to do exercises without fail. Then clean out garage. Job must be finished before Dad gets home. Mark to fill holes and rake under pine tree after swimming class.' "

The last bite of hot dog stuck in Mark's throat. Swimming class—that's what he'd forgotten.

Kelli stared at him. "You're not supposed to be here. I'd hate to be in your shoes when Mom finds out you've skipped class again."

"I forgot," Mark mumbled.

"It's easy to forget things you don't want to remember."

Kelli was right. From the beginning, when Mom enrolled him in the Minnows group, he had dreaded the class. At the first lesson he had shivered at poolside while little first-graders swam to the ladder and climbed out. Water had streamed down their baby-fat legs, and their suits were hardly big enough to display Tadpole,

Aquatot, and Polywog patches they had already earned.

Boys who had started class with Mark soon swam away as Fish, then dived as Flying Fish. They became Sharks, and some now cut the water as Porpoises. Mark was still a choking, threshing Minnow in a class with six-year-old drips, who stared up at the big one in their midst.

The swimming instructor looked at him, too, in a grim way and said, "Frye, I've never had a kid I couldn't teach to swim, and you're not going to spoil my record."

Mark thought of Zanzutu children, all of whom could swim at birth. He seldom mentioned swimming class at home. He knew every kid was supposed to love water and a chance to swim.

Kelli turned her attention from Mark to Scott, who lay motionless on his stomach on the living-room floor. "Way to exercise, Scott. You'll never get your back straightened that way. Dr. Feluchi said you were getting worse. Mom thinks you'll be in for a big operation if you don't do your back exercises. Better finish your workout, then blitz the garage."

"Shut up." Scott's voice was muffled in the shag rug. He raised his head. "How about you? What are you supposed to do?"

"Listen here, Scott. I put in a four-hour shift at Charley's Chicken. Then I went by Rex-Tech and put in a job application."

"What did they say?" Mark asked.

"Same old thing. They're not taking anybody who

hasn't graduated from high school. Some kind of company rule."

Scott propped his head on his big hands. "It's your own fault, Kelli. If you'd stayed in school and graduated the way Mom and Dad told you instead of running off with the worst punk in Hardin Grove, you'd be sitting pretty right now. Maybe be a foreman down at Rex-Tech."

Now it was Kelli's turn to yell at Scott to shut up. She grabbed her old oil-stained jacket and slammed the door when she went outside. Mark took another hot dog, went into the living room, and sat on the sofa.

"Get off my cap," Scott ordered.

Mark shifted and pulled out from under him a green cap with "John Deere" printed in yellow on its high crown. Scott was never far from that cap. Mark measured him with his eye as Scott lay on the floor. Scott's big feet in blue-and-white running shoes were a long way from his head of wavy brown hair. He was at least as tall as Dad.

Scott looked up from under heavy brows that continued in a few stray hairs over the bridge of his nose. "Well, are you waiting for the show to start?"

"Uh-huh. I just wondered what the doctor thought."

"Mom will give you bulletins on that every hour, on the hour."

Scott began to do push-ups, fast at first, then more slowly. He changed to a head-back, knees-straight, feet-up exercise that formed his long body into a curve. He groaned, grunted, and finally lay still as if exhausted.

Mark thought of the exercise instruction sheet that was taped to the refrigerator door. "Want me to get your exercise list so you'll know what comes next?"

Scott panted. "I know what comes next. Listen, Mark, since you skipped swim class again, why don't you start filling up those holes like Mom said?"

"Can't. You have to clean out the garage first so I can find the shovel."

Scott sat up. Slowly he raised and lowered each leg thirty times.

"Are your exercises hard?" Mark asked.

"Some are; some aren't. But they are all super boring. It's no fun doing this stuff alone every day and having everybody yell at me if I happen to take time out for a minute or so once in a while."

"Maybe I could help you. Be like a coach," Mark suggested.

"Naw, Mark. It's my back. I'll do it. I wish you'd stop sitting there staring at me. Why don't you try to train Ozro or go see Mrs. McSwiggen, your old-lady girlfriend?"

Before Scott could do any more teasing, Mark went outside and wandered around the yard. The plastic sheet covering Scott's motorcycle billowed and crackled in the wind. He hadn't worked on his Honda for months. Scott had paid fifty-three dollars of his newspaper delivery money for that wrecked Honda. At his present rate he'd have his driver's license before he had the motorcycle running.

Mark moved the plastic and sat on the cycle. He missed working on it with Scott. Maybe Scott connected both Mark and the motorcycle with the bad day last summer when his back problem was discovered.

Mark remembered how hot it had been that day, even in the shade where Scott was bent over the trail bike 90. Scott had worn cutoff jeans and had tied his long hair back with a shoestring to keep it out of his eyes. Suddenly the motor had fired, and both Scott and Mark had cheered throughout the seven seconds it ran.

"You're getting it, Scott!" Mark had shouted.

"Yeah. Well, that's enough for today. It's too hot to work." Scott had pulled off his sweaty T-shirt.

That's when Mark had noticed that one side of Scott's chest was sunken. He reached out to touch him. "What's wrong with your chest?"

Scott had stepped away. "Nothin'. Look out. It's too hot." But Scott himself had looked shocked when he ran his hand across his chest.

Mom did all the talking a few days later, after she and Scott had seen Dr. Feluchi. Scott's chest was all right; the trouble was his back. He was growing tall so fast that his back muscles didn't support his backbone. As his spine shifted to the side, it pulled his chest muscles with it.

If Scott exercised faithfully to strengthen his back muscles, he would be able to avoid wearing a heavy brace or having an operation that would put him in a cast for months. Those exercises were important.

At first Scott didn't miss a day. Then the exercises he was supposed to do became harder and the job more annoying. He didn't want any of his friends to know he had back trouble and always stopped exercising if they came by. When Mom went to school to find out why he'd gotten an *F* in phys ed, she learned he'd stopped dressing for gym.

Scott often skipped exercising for days and always complained of the drudgery. The more Mom prodded him, the more sullen he became. Mom complained to Dad, when he was home, of Scott's slacking. But Dad couldn't help much when he was on the highway hauling lettuce.

The squeak of a car hood hinge turned Mark's attention to the back of the yard, where Kelli bent over the engine of a rusted Chrysler with flat tires. He kicked at dry weed stalks as he went to the car with a smashed rear end. "Kelli, Mrs. McSwiggen wants to know when you're getting this junker out of here. She says it makes the neighborhood look bad."

Kelli tried to loosen a nut. "Prissy old dame. Doesn't know the difference between a parts car and a junker. I might put another good parts car back here. Then I'll take the motor of our car down to the block and rebuild it. I sure wish I could afford an impact wrench to loosen these nuts."

"I'd like to be as good as you are at motors and machines," Mark said.

"Before Dad bought the truck and went on the road, I used to watch and help him fix cars. That's what we did," Kelli explained.

"I'll bet you're smarter than a lot of people with high school diplomas."

Kelli straightened up. "I can't prove it. I was AT, though, from seventh grade until ninth."

"What's AT?"

"Academically Talented, Mark. Haven't you kids in fifth grade heard about it yet? Well, in junior high, you have these advanced classes for bright kids who get good grades. But even with AT, I guess you can't tell how far a person will go or in what direction." With a tissue from her jacket pocket Kelli wiped her nose. "I guess I took the wrong direction. Dropout, that's an awful label."

Mark looked at the car motor and wondered how he'd explain the internal-combustion engine to the Zanzutus. "Kelli, how would you show people who didn't know anything about modern stuff—motors, TV, computers—how it all worked?"

Kelli bent over the engine. "Get an old model and take it apart, I guess."

"But if there weren't any old ones left anywhere."

"That's not likely. People are always throwing things away," Kelli said.

"But what if there weren't any dumps or anything?" Mark leaned over beside her so she'd be sure to hear.

"Mark, will you get out of the way? There's little enough room here for me to get this corroded nut loose." She stood back, wiping her hands on a rag. "Why are you asking all these dumb questions?"

"Sometimes I get to thinking what if I was the only—" He stopped. Kelli would think he was far from AT.

She turned to look at him and then smoothed his hair down over his ears. "Evening sun is shining through your ears. It's too late now, but I should have taped your ears down at night when you were a baby. Now why don't you go play with the Skinner boys?"

Mark didn't answer. She might as well have suggested that he go play with a couple of rabid bats.

"Or you could help Scott. Start cleaning the garage while he does his exercises," Kelli said.

"Have you looked in there lately?" Mark asked. "It's really awesome."

"Fill up those holes then. Mom won't be so sore at you for skipping swim class if you do that."

Mark went to the tree in the side yard and studied the bare roots and holes beneath it. A plastic bulldozer had lost its blade. A rusting metal high-lift loader lay across a ditch. An overturned dump truck was minus a wheel. It was a disaster area.

He looked into the nearby garage. A table made from an old door set on carpenter's horses was piled high with paint cans, dried-out paintbrushes and rollers, empty glass jars, egg cartons, and flowerpots complete with dead plants. Scrap lumber was piled beneath the table; lawn chairs were stored in front of it. The lawn mower and snowblower were wedged behind it. A tangle of tool handles leaned against an old desk at the back of the garage. Brooms, mops, pails, baskets, and a broken ski were cluttered against the walls.

Mark was wondering where to start when he saw Mrs. McSwiggen drive home. If he helped her unload what she'd bought at the auction, she might take him to the Y. The swimming instructor had said he'd give Mark extra help anytime. Mom would be mighty pleased to know he was making up the classes she'd paid for.

CHAPTER THREE

As Mark ran by the pine tree, he caught a glimpse of Scott's bright green and yellow cap in the dark branches. "What are you doing up there?"

"Thinking about starting my job." Scott's voice had a strange way of wobbling up and down.

"If you find the shovel, put it by my old interstate," Mark called back. He and Ozro headed for Mrs. McSwiggen's.

Her house had been a one-room school. Mrs. McSwiggen often boasted of walking miles in all kinds of weather when she was a little girl to just such a building. Frequently she reminded Mark to be grateful for the school bus. He thought it would be better to flounder through snowdrifts to school instead of being battered at the bus stop.

From Mrs. McSwiggen Mark had learned to identify other one-room schoolhouses around the countryside. Some were tumbling down. Others had become remodeled homes, garages, fast-food stands, or barns. Mrs. McSwiggen's place still looked like a schoolhouse. It had two front doors—one for boys, one for girls. Three identical windows on one side faced three on the other. Mrs. McSwiggen had neither front nor back windows, no back door, and no porches. She did her own painting and kept the place sparkling white, including the bell cupola on the tin roof. She retouched the letters of the oval sign on the front gable that read: HARDIN CREEK SCHOOL DISTRICT 81, 1848. Her paintbrush couldn't conceal the deep gouges on one door, which she claimed was the boys' entrance. She used the woodshed for a garage and the sunny part of the playground for a vegetable garden.

Mrs. McSwiggen clutched the mail she'd just taken from her box. "Come on inside out of this wind, Mark. Let's see what I've got here."

As they went in, she glanced at a long envelope. "Oh, another one of those letters. That'll go right out with the junk mail. Not much first-class mail. Not a first-class day, either, standing in the wind at the auction. I got a few things, though."

"I'll help you unload," Mark offered. "Then I sure wish I could get a ride to the Y. I forgot to go to swimming class."

"I guess we could work that out. Let me get warm first."

Someone knocked on the girls' door. They knew it was a stranger, for that door was blocked with boxes of things Mrs. McSwiggen had bought at household sales.

The visitor looked startled when the door he had not knocked on opened. "Edna McSwiggen?" he asked as he came to the right entrance and handed her a little white card.

Mrs. McSwiggen nodded and fluffed her wig. The wind mussed the stranger's hair and billowed his topcoat as he waited for her to compare his card with the long envelope she fished out of her wastebasket.

"Young man, do you have anything to do with this mall business?" Mrs. McSwiggen seemed ready to shut the door in his face, but he stood in the entrance.

"Yes, as you see I'm with Distribution Development, Site Acquisition Department. I've been trying to get hold of you. Been here a dozen times and didn't catch you in. I want to talk to you personally to coordinate our schedule with the move you'll be making from our property here."

"Your property!" Mrs. McSwiggen gasped. "You'd better come in the rest of the way so I can explain a few things to you. Show you a copy of my deed and my tax receipts."

The man made a dry sound that was supposed to be a chuckle. "That won't be necessary. We always try to be helpful in cases of premises vacating."

"Vacating, my foot!" Mrs. McSwiggen glared at him.

"Your computer that writes me those ridiculous letters is haywire. Tell the mall people their computer is down."

The man was no longer smiling. "You ignored our repeated written offers of cooperation."

"I haven't sold an inch of this property to anybody," Mrs. McSwiggen stated firmly.

"That's because you have nothing to sell." The man raised his voice. "We've checked all records in your case and have completed our legal requirements."

Mark hissed at Ozro, hoping he'd growl at the intruder, but Ozro continued to wag his tail.

"Since you refuse to cooperate, Mrs. McSwiggen, you leave Distribution Development no choice except to maintain our demolition schedule." The man turned to leave. Mark was pleased that Ozro's friendly leap left muddy footprints on the man's topcoat.

"We'll just see about that." Mrs. McSwiggen closed the door and glanced up at the big schoolroom clock on the wall. "We can still get to the courthouse before closing time. I've got copies of my deed and tax payment receipts right here handy. Come on, Mark. Where was it you wanted to go?"

"Swimming," Mark almost whispered. "But what's this all about? What does that guy want?"

"Oh, not much," she said as they went outside. "Just the roof over my head and my future profitable business."

She backed the station wagon halfway down the drive

and pointed to a space between the two doors. "That's where I planned to have a neat eye-catching sign— SCHOOLHOUSE ANTIQUES. I thought maybe I'd get your mom to letter it for me. Not like that thing, big as a boxcar." She tossed her head toward a weather-beaten sign in the open tract adjoining her house on the south.

The sign had been there a long time: COMING SOON. HARDIN GROVE MALL. THIRTY-FIVE SPECIALTY SHOPS. TWO DEPARTMENT STORES. DISTRIBUTION DEVELOPMENT, INC.

"At first I thought there was nothing to it." Mrs. McSwiggen shook her head. "Way out here on the old Hardin dairy farm. But it's getting closer, as you heard. You can't tell town from country anymore. They want half of Hardin Township for a parking lot. From where their stakes were with their little orange flags, I figured they were coming right to my property line. I thought I'd just have to make the best of it. You can't stop progress.

"I even thought it would be all to the good." She nudged Mark. "With five acres of asphalt so close, folks would have a handy place to park. They could step right over to my place for some real interesting shopping. But then one day I saw those little orange flags over here on this side, between my place and yours."

Mark looked out the car window. "Where? I don't see any."

"That's because I pulled 'em up and threw 'em away. They were way out of line. Next thing you know people were tramping around my property, trespassing, surveyors and men with clipboards. Not even a word to me. Then those letters started. The latest ones claim I'm trespassing on their property, but they'll be nice, let me stay rent-free a day or so until I relocate so they can knock the place down."

"Knock it down!" Mark was appalled. "They can't do that."

"Of course not. Just when I'm about ready to open my business. I've been to every household sale, every auction hereabouts for years, gathering my stock. Having a business would be company for me. Lots of nice folks dropping in." She bit her lip. "It's been lonely without Shorty."

Mrs. McSwiggen had been a widow so long that Mark couldn't remember Shorty. Once she'd told him she'd refused chances to marry again because she was afraid she'd get a lemon.

"Shorty, I may have to give up my dream." She seemed to have forgotten that Mark was right beside her.

"Can they help you at the courthouse?" Mark's question brought her back to the present.

"Sure, if we get a payday move on." They started for Hardin Grove.

CHAPTER FOUR

T he red-brick courthouse topped with a fancy dome was flanked by two low additions with lots of big windows. Mrs. McSwiggen knew right where to go and led the way along a dark corridor in the old part of the building.

"Somehow Max Bookout got himself elected register and recorder," she said. "I went to high school with him. He sure wasn't the smartest one in the class." She turned into an office, where she refused to state her business to the receptionist and demanded to see Max Bookout. "I help pay his salary," she declared.

Max Bookout, smoking a cigar, strolled out of his inner office. "Well, Edna, you finally got here and brought Sonny along." Mark dodged so he wouldn't be patted on the head. "You should have come sooner. The mall people are way ahead of you. They've been all over our maps and records like a wet circus tent."

"I had other things to do. But now I want to put a stop to this nonsense." Mrs. McSwiggen waved the copy of her deed. "You know Shorty and I bought the Hardin Creek School building when the directors finally decided to close their school and go in with the big township district. Hardin Creek was the last one-room school in the county. We paid cash, and they gave us this deed."

"Right as rain, Edna. Only trouble is some folks didn't do their homework on that school business. Edna, you've got a flaw in your title." Max Bookout's hand shook a little as he held it up to stop Mrs. McSwiggen's protests. "Come on down to the map room in the basement. I'll show you the situation."

They went into a musty-smelling room. Max Bookout wheezed and puffed as he took a heavy volume of maps down from a shelf and spread it open on a long table. The map on the big page was marked into different-sized areas labeled with family names that Mark recognized.

"Right here on this plat map, where we mark who owns what, it shows that the Hardin tract, whole kit and caboodle, belongs to the mall company now." Max puffed on his cigar.

Mrs. McSwiggen fanned smoke from her face. "Where does it show my property?"

Mr. Bookout used the chewed end of his cigar for a pointer. "Ought to be right here, but it's not." Mark saw

"Frye" lettered in a small rectangle near Max Bookout's cigar.

He tried hard to follow Max's explanation. The Hardins, who were early settlers, owned lots of land. When more families came, there was need for a public school, so one was built beside the road on land off the Hardin holdings. Everybody must have supposed the Hardins had given the land for a school, but the early school directors had not bothered to get a deed as proof.

Years later other directors decided a deed might come in handy. They drew one up stating the property belonged to the school district since it had held undisputed possession and made use of the property for the time required by law to establish ownership.

"Squatter's right law. That's what they used," Mr. Bookout said. "That was easier than trying to find out if the land was ever donated. Lots less trouble than tracking down scattered Hardins and getting them to quit claims. But the worst part is that when the deed was recorded, no one ever marked on the map that the school ground was split from the big Hardin tract."

Mrs. McSwiggen was scornful. "Some lummox too lazy to dip a pen in ink and mark off a few scratches."

"Sloppy work way back then," Mr. Bookout admitted. "The Hardins had so much land that they didn't realize the school's two acres were included in their tax payments. It wasn't much, but they paid it all those years."

Mrs. McSwiggen tapped the paper she held. "Anyhow, this deed is good. That's for sure."

Mr. Bookout shook his head. "Not according to the mall lawyers. I wouldn't put it past them to claim that the Hardins never gave up the school land since they kept paying taxes on it. They might say that payment was the Hardins' way of disputing the school's right to possession. That's where your title flaw is, Edna.

"When you and Shorty bought the place, the directors gave you their deed, but once again the map wasn't marked. Ordinarily that negligence is corrected at tax time when the past owner and the new owner both get a bill for the same property. The past owner raises an awful fuss here at the courthouse, and everything is straightened out. In your case, the past owner was a school district. Schools aren't taxed, so the directors didn't get a bill and we didn't get any complaints."

Mrs. McSwiggen straightened her shoulders. "Shorty and I paid our taxes. Good years and bad."

"Oh, I know. You might have a fightin' chance if you had lived there long enough to have squatter's right yourself. You're a little bit shy." Mr. Bookout puffed hard on his cigar to get it going again. "As it is, I don't think you've got a leg to stand on. It's late, but you can get yourself a lawyer. Maybe he'll find you a loophole. I'm surprised a sharp person like you didn't see the legal ads that ran in the paper. It was in three times: Anyone having claims on the Hardin land was warned to speak up within twenty days. The whole thing was spelled out."

Mrs. McSwiggen was shocked speechless. Her steps dragged as she and Mark left the courthouse. Mark hurried ahead to get out in the fresh air. He had to remind her where she'd parked the station wagon. The time didn't seem right to ask her to take him to the Y. Anyhow, the swimming teacher had probably gone home to dinner.

"Max Bookout! He always was about as careful as a cyclone." Mrs. McSwiggen's spunk seemed to return as they drove out of Hardin Grove. "He could have caught that mistake long ago."

"Are you mad at Max?"

"Not as mad as I am at myself. I should have read the legal notices on the classified page of the *Herald* instead of all those ads for garage sales and auctions. I'll tell you, Mark, it's hard to know what's important and what's unimportant in this world."

"How could marks on an old map mean more than you do, a flesh-and-blood lady living in her schoolhouse? I don't get it."

"It takes a legal mind, whatever that is," she said.

"Mr. Bookout said you could get a lawyer," Mark reminded her. "Maybe he could find a loophole where you could stand on one leg."

"I'll have to stop buying, start selling if I do. Lawyers don't come cheap. I've got a cash-flow problem." Mrs.

McSwiggen drove in silence for a while. "Grand Canyon!" she suddenly exclaimed. "I don't care; I'm glad we went. Oh, that was a wonderful sight."

She wasn't making much sense. Mark thought the threat of loss of her home had been too much for her. "What about Grand Canyon?"

"That's where we went. After Shorty put in his thirty years at the plant, we sold our big house and traveled out to the West for six months. Then we came back and bought the little school. So we don't quite have the twenty years' ownership to give squatter's right." She made a face in distaste. "Squatter sounds so undignified. Like a rag-tag outfit without a change of clothes or a chair to sit on."

"I've got it," Mark said. "Get the Hardins to say they gave the land to the school. Wouldn't that be easy?"

"No, it wouldn't, considering the Hardin that gave the land back in the eighteen hundreds somewhere has been in the Hardin Cemetery for more than a hundred years. Hardins, their in-laws, outlaws, and shirttail relations are scattered all over creation. They don't care two pins for Hardin Township and were glad to sell their land here."

Mrs. McSwiggen glanced over at Mark. "Oh, heavens! I forgot to take you wherever it was you wanted to go. Shall we go back?"

Mark told her he had a big job waiting for him at home and that he didn't mind missing swim class. They drove by a field with a row of mobile homes along one side. He supposed each family paid a fee to park there. How would he explain the landownership system to the Zanzutus? They doubtless considered everything in the radius of a three-day run the tribe's hunting ground.

"Mrs. McSwiggen, suppose you knew about something but didn't know exactly how it worked, but you had to teach somebody, what would you do?"

"Look it up somewhere. There's a set of the *Book of Knowledge* right here in back. I bought it today along with a lot of old books." But in the world Mark tried to imagine there would be no books, old or new. "I wish I hadn't spent a red cent," she confided. "Now I'd like to sell what I spent cash for today."

They passed a house with a garage sale sign in the yard. Mark thought of the cluttered Frye garage. "I've got an idea for you. We can sell some of your stuff at our garage sale. We're going to have one Saturday."

CHAPTER FIVE

Mark was proud of himself for thinking of a garage sale on the spur of the moment. Mrs. McSwiggen, who was pleased to take part in the event, drove directly to the Fryes'. Mark staggered under the weight of a box of books that he carried to the garage.

Mrs. McSwiggen came puffing with another box. "I musta bought a whole library. Might be something good in here, but let somebody else look." Still, after she had put the box down, she inspected several. "You can tell a lot about people from the books they leave behind: what they studied, their hopes, what they liked to do, things that worried them, even the diseases they had."

As Mark lugged boxes, he thought about the Zanzutus, who couldn't read. He'd have to teach them, and that would be some job, considering he didn't understand their language. He made grunting sounds and tried to figure out how to spell them.

Somehow Mrs. McSwiggen had managed to get into her station wagon a piece of furniture that looked worthless to Mark. He volunteered Scott's help to get it out. However, Mrs. McSwiggen didn't want to unload the dry sink, which she considered too good for a garage sale. She'd waited all day for the auctioneer to put it up and then had to take it along with a weight-lifting set, which he couldn't sell otherwise. She planned now to take the wooden sink to the flea market where she had decided to rent sales space. But Mark knew unloading those weights could be a problem. Iron disks and a polished metal bar lay along the side of the cargo space.

"There's a wheelbarrow way back in the garage," Mark said.

Mrs. McSwiggen shook her head. "Be like pulling a tooth to get it out."

Mark called to Scott, who came to the side door but made no move to help. "We're making your job easier, Scott." Mark was enthusiastic.

Scott wasn't. He looked at the growing piles of bags and boxes. "Some way," he said. Mark changed his mind about asking him to help.

Mom was puzzled when she pulled into the driveway bordered with castoffs. "It's for Saturday," Mark announced. "Our garage sale. I'm helping Scott. Quickest way to clear out the place. We're going to sell stuff for

Mrs. McSwiggen, too." He started collecting broken toys from under the pine tree. "Some of these need a little fixing, but they'll sell. Then I can fill in these holes."

"Hi, neighbor," Mom said as she got out of the car. "I haven't seen you lately. How is everything?"

"Not too good. I've just had a day; I'm about tuckered out." She tossed a coconut shell carved to resemble a monkey into a bag of knickknacks. "I hope Mark is right saying I can put some choice items in your sale. It's much appreciated just now, I'll tell you."

"I had thought about a sale, later maybe. I hadn't decided." Mom moved a heavy leather suitcase out of the way. "I don't know about this Saturday. Only four days away. Then, too, there's a conference that day at the YW called 'Careers for Later Years.' I can't miss that. You know I want to get my ducks in a row. Give something my best shot. Most of my friends have gone back to work. I'd sure like to be on a payroll."

Mark tried to push an armful of toys into the garage. "We can't get everything in here. We'd better have the sale Saturday before a big rain comes. I can run it, Mom. Scott can help, maybe even Kelli. I'll mark your stuff with yellow stickers, Mrs. McSwiggen."

"I'd love to help," Mrs. McSwiggen said, "but I've made up my mind to rent sales space at the fire hall flea market. Come Saturday, I'll be down there selling at my booth. I can't let one of those markets go by."

Mom skirted the uneven ground around the pine tree as she went toward the side door. "If the public is coming in here for a sale, Mark, you've got to fill these holes. If somebody fell, we could have a lawsuit against us. I'll take a look inside. See what else I can round up."

So it was settled. Mom had agreed to Saturday's sale. Mark could hear her opening kitchen cabinets, looking for stock, as he helped Mrs. McSwiggen finish unloading. Together they managed to roll the weights out one at a time.

After Mrs. McSwiggen had left, Mark started clearing space on the garage table. He had a place ready when Mom came out with a pair of laced ski boots, an unstrung tennis racket, a picnic basket with a broken handle, and a Chinese back scratcher.

"What's this, Mom?" Mark held up an aluminum bowl with a dangling electric cord.

"Gadget to keep dinner rolls hot. It's too much fuss to plug in a separate appliance to warm rolls. Put it in the sale."

Scott, who had been giving Mark advice but no help, retrieved a soft, deflating basketball from a pile of discards. "You can leave this out."

Scott no longer practiced shots into the hoop on the garage gable. "You don't use it anymore," Mark said.

Scott threw the logy ball back into the garage. "It's still my ball."

Mom studied Scott for a moment. "Did you finish all your exercises? Dr. Feluchi said we didn't improve any and if we—"

"Where do you get that *we* stuff?" Scott interrupted. "It's my back. I was there. Remember? You don't have to ask me every commercial break if I did those dumb exercises. I'm doin' 'em."

"All right, Scott, all right." Mom was impatient. "It's for your own good."

Scott bent over and held his stomach. "Dinner would be for my own good right now."

Mom stepped over a stack of plastic egg cartons. "After sampling all that cake icing, I'm not very hungry. I guess I'll just fix a big salad for dinner."

"And what else?" Scott implored as he followed her into the kitchen.

Mark was glad he had hidden the last two raw hot dogs behind a pickle jar in the refrigerator. He was sticking a toy tractor wheel on with electrical tape when Kelli came out. "I hear we're having a garage sale Saturday," she said between sneezes. "Who are you trying to fool with broken junk like that?"

"Nobody," Mark asserted. "I'll mark it 'as is.' That takes care of everything."

From a pile of castoffs, Kelli retrieved a refrigerator vegetable crisper. "Don't you dare sell this pan. I use it when I change motor oil." She put the pan on the highest garage shelf. "Nothing is safe. Mom's going over the whole house. No time to make dinner. She told me to fix a salad. I have to go to the grocery store for the makings."

Since Kelli had reduced his stock, Mark decided to slip into her room to see if she had something she might as well get rid of. It was the neatest room in the house. Mark had never seen her bed unmade and wondered if a girl could make her bed while she was still in it.

He opened her closet, where her clean Charley's Chicken uniform hung ready for the next shift. On a shelf far back in the gloom of the closet he made out the shapes of carefully placed stuffed toys. He brought worn and soiled dogs, cats, monkeys, and elephants out to the light. Kelli certainly didn't need them anymore.

She'd probably had them in her closet because she was embarrassed to have them still. They'd make little kids happy. A good garage sale included lots of toys. Without them children whined to leave, and their parents didn't stay long enough to buy anything.

He examined a bear that was worn almost hairless. The little faded label hanging from its side read: "Cuddle Toys, Inc., outer cover: 100% cotton, filling: unknown fiber." Unknown fiber! Other toys had similar labels. Right there in her own room Kelli had a stack of unknown fibers. Some of it was leaking out of the worn toys. Mark was sure he'd found the cause of her allergy.

He'd do her a favor and put those critters with unknown stuffing in the sale. He could ask her, but she might be softhearted about her old toys. Best to get rid of them. She'd thank him later. Mark went to the kitchen for a black plastic garbage bag.

As he filled the big bag, he wondered about the Cuddle Toys factory. Maybe the workers saved the floor sweepings at the end of the day for stuffing toys the next day.

Mark left the bag in the hall and went into his parents' room when he heard Mom rummaging there.

"With my blow dryer and new permanent I don't need those." Mom pointed to about a half bushel of pink plastic curlers on the bed. "Now that I'm into cake decorating, I'll never finish making this latch-hook rug." The bag of bright yarn she tossed to the bed slid off the pile of curlers. "Your dad will be glad to see more room in here. This is supposed to be the master bedroom." Mom shook her head. "Mostly the master sleeps in his truck."

Mom unplugged a light that stood on her crowded night table. When it was turned on, red globs like clotted blood floated in the liquid of the globe. "Dad got this at a truck stop gift shop. I never liked it. He won't miss it. Let's sell it."

Mark intended to price it low. It had to sell. That light had always made him a little sick.

Mom searched drawers. "A person needs to clear things out."

Mark thought of the Zanzutu custom. At this time of year they had big parties to feast on the last of their stored food. Then they threw into the cooking fires everything else they had. Finally they burned down their huts. The Great Burning Festival of the Zanzutus would be in about a week, when the tribe was sure the days were longer than the nights. That called for celebration. By getting rid of everything, the Zanzutus showed faith that they could get it all back again in the coming long, sunny days.

Mark thought the Zanzutus went too far when they burned their homes. He'd have to instruct them in the value of keeping a roof over their heads.

"Mom, if you wanted to know something, so you could teach somebody all about it, what would you do?"

"I suppose I'd take a course at the Y. They have all kinds of classes." Mention of the Y reminded Mom of something. "How did swimming class go today, Mark?"

"All right, I guess." He didn't feel good about his answer, even though it was true, sort of. He imagined class had gone all right. That was his best guess, and the instructor was probably glad Mark hadn't come to remind him that he wasn't a perfect teacher.

"Did you get a ride home with someone from class?"

"With a friend." That answer was true, too, sort of. Mrs. McSwiggen was certainly a friend. He'd doubtless been a help going with her to the courthouse.

"I saw your instructor on the street last week, and he said he'd never—"

"Mom, listen," Mark interrupted. "Mrs. McSwiggen has a flaw in her title. She may not have a leg to stand on. I just happen to know."

Leaving out how he just happened to know, Mark told of Mrs. McSwiggen's plight. Mom stopped rummaging and really listened. She was dismayed at Mark's news. "It could be the high rise for the elderly for her. That is, if she can get in. I've heard they have a waiting list for those little broom-closet apartments. She'll miss her garden, and you know she's a regular pack rat. I should have realized something was wrong if she wanted to get rid of any of her treasures. She said things weren't too good. With her that means they are downright dismal.

"It's a shame." Mom opened another drawer. "Now there's a woman who has plans, knows what she wants to do. Not like me. Trying one thing, then another. Linda Frye. Sputtering around like a hot skillet. Mark, here's something else for the sale. I didn't finish these elves I started in ceramics class."

Mark tucked the box of half-painted clay figurines under one arm, the light under the other, and still managed to drag out the bag of stuffed toys. He met Kelli coming in the side door. She glanced at the box and the light, pronounced them good riddance, and ignored the bulging black bag.

The light of the vernal equinox day was fading. It was getting colder, too. Mark pulled up the hood of his jacket and turned on the garage light so he could inspect the old books. There were plenty with fine print and few pictures but not one about tribes in remote places.

He came across *The One-Volume Encyclopedia of Sports*. Its jacket design was alive with swimmers, runners, and boxers. All were smiling winners. Nothing looked hard. An archer hit the bull's-eye. Each boxer fought only one opponent.

Mark pretended that a slab of crumbling foam rubber nearby was Jack Skinner and threw a few punches at it. He wheeled and jabbed at an imagined La Vern. With flailing arms he fought both off at once. He held up his arm in victory, then turned again to the sports book.

Swimming looked so easy. The diagrams sketched various strokes. None showed the no-form struggle needed just to keep from drowning. There were no slow learners, no chokers.

Weight lifting was described near the back of the encyclopedia. The diagram figures of lifters were larger and more powerful than those of any other sport shown. Weight lifting didn't seem to require much skill, and it promised brute strength. That's what Mark needed to lick the Skinners. The same strong muscles would doubtless make him an outstanding swimmer. The instructor would apologize to him and put him on the Y swim team. Mark pawed the air in a crawl stroke.

He stopped to study a back view of a smooth-muscled lifter. Weight lifting would benefit Scott, too. It sure would be fun to work with him on something again. If

Scott wasn't nagged to do those boring exercises alone, he'd stop being grumpy.

One step back, and Mark would fall over all the weight-lifting equipment they needed. It was right there by their own garage. He located a piece of cardboard, wrote "sold" on it, and taped it to the shining bar of the set.

Scott seemed to think his back problem was his alone, so Mark knew he'd have to approach him carefully. When he went inside, he made a quick grab into the refrigerator as he went through the kitchen.

Scott was reclining on the living-room floor. "Haven't you finished your exercises yet?" Mark asked.

"Yeah, but I'm about to pass out from hunger."

Mark gave him a hot dog. "This will give you strength to sit up. I'll bet you didn't do them all."

Scott finished the hot dog in two bites. "Listen, Mark, for a guy who forgets swimming class—"

"We've already sold something, Scott. Those weights Mrs. McSwiggen put in the sale."

"Who bought them?"

"We did," Mark announced.

"Who's we?"

"You and I. We'll work out with them together."

"Yeah? What did *we* use for money? A set of weights is worth something."

"They're secondhand," Mark pointed out.

"Mark, you can't do much to wear out cast-iron weights."

"I figured you had money from delivering papers, Scott."

"And I've got better things to do with my dough." Scott put his cap squarely on his head.

"I'll have plenty of cash after the sale. I'll buy them, but I'll need you to help me use them."

"Naw, Mark, I've got better things to do with my time."

Mark gave him a second hot dog. "Think about it anyhow."

From the kitchen Kelli announced that her super chef salad was served. Mark beat Scott to the table.

CHAPTER SIX

eturning from school the next day, Mark held to the side of the seat as the bus driver swung around potholes in the road. He was eager to get home. Maybe, just maybe, Scott was already setting up the big sale. When he bounded off the bus at the Frye mailbox, he saw the mess around the garage just as it had been the previous evening. Scott had not done one thing to get ready. He was home, though. Mark saw Scott's cap in the pine tree.

"Hey, Scott," Mark called up to him. "We have to put prices on everything for Saturday's sale. Aren't you going to help? It's already Wednesday."

"Might," Scott answered, but he didn't come down.

Mark wanted company while he worked. Using Scott's footholds, he climbed the tree trunk and pulled himself up through the prickly pine needles to a limb beside

Scott. "It's nice once you get up here." He took a deep breath. "It smells good."

"It's private, most of the time." Scott looked closely at Mark. "Where did you get the fat lip?"

Mark winced when he touched his lip. He had thought the swelling from Jack Skinner's morning punch would be gone. "Musta run into something."

"Like somebody's fist?" Scott asked. "And your shirt pocket is ripped."

"Ozro is always jumping up on me with his big claws."

"You ought to train your dog, Mark."

"I can't now. We have to get ready for the big sale. Come on, Scott."

"I can't hang around with a fifth grader all the time," Scott said. "You won't even tell me the truth about your fat lip. Get some kids your own age to have a sale with you."

Mark pretended to search in the tree branches. "Where'll I get 'em? I don't see any. The only kids in the neighborhood now are the Skinners."

"What about them? Their place down on the creek looks like a landfill. They'd have plenty to put in a sale."

Mark squirmed on the limb. "Jack and La Vern are bossy."

"Nobody's perfect," Scott reminded him.

Mark felt his lip. "I know, but they're not my friends."

Mark considered boys his age in the Zanzutu tribe. They all went around together in a pack, hunting, fishing, and learning to fight other tribes. They never fought one another. Friendship was so natural among all Zanzutus that they didn't even think about it.

Scott flicked Mark's tattered shirt pocket. "No dog did that."

Mark started to climb down. "Let's price for the sale. Then you can help me work out with that weight-lifting set."

"Why should I, when you won't tell me who socked you and ripped your good school shirt? Why is it top secret?"

Mark picked at a bit of bark. "Not top secret. Not even bottom secret."

"Well, get on down. Mom wants you to fill up those holes under this tree."

Mark rubbed a sprig of pine between his fingers. It was nice up there in the sweet-smelling greenness close to his brother. Scott hadn't talked to him so much for a long time. Through the limbs he could see the stacks in and around the garage. If he worked alone, most of the sale money would be his. He'd have unlimited funds to play Space Invaders at the game arcade. But the mess below looked so dismal, he didn't want to tackle the job alone. Being rich wasn't enough. He needed company.

"It's the Skinners," Mark blurted out. "They jump me at the bus stop. I'll do well to live until school's out." He rushed on to tell Scott of all he had suffered.

Scott gave a low whistle and pushed his cap to the back of his head. "Sounds like the Skinners are trying to skin you alive. All you do is try to dodge 'em."

"Maybe they'll move away to the Sunbelt," Mark said hopefully.

"More likely more Skinners will pile in there with them. No, Mark, you'll have to stop hiding and take a stand."

"There are two of them," Mark pointed out.

"Makes no difference."

"It does to me," Mark said.

"You need confidence, Mark. Get the right attitude, and you can spoil their fun."

"Attitude!" Mark exclaimed. He was ready to comment on Scott's climb-a-tree attitude when urged to do his exercises. But nagging wasn't part of his sneaky plan to help both Scott and himself. Instead, Mark lifted his arm and tried to bulge a bicep. "I need muscle, too. That's why I want you to work out with me on the weights. We'll get more than enough from our sale to pay Mrs. McSwiggen for them."

Before Scott could agree, Kelli came out of the house, calling, "Scott, Mom says get in here and do your exercises." She looked toward the pine. "You won't believe this, Mom," she shouted, "but they are both up in that tree."

They were soon down. Scott reminded Kelli that he'd

been told to get the garage in order. He couldn't do but one thing at a time. He'd do those stupid exercises after he had helped Mark.

Kelli looked over sale items as if ready to snatch back anything she wanted to keep. Her eyes were still red, but Mark supposed an allergy stopped gradually. He was glad the bag of stuffed toys was wedged under a rickety kitchen stool.

Mark felt better after telling Scott his troubles. He hummed as he arranged and priced books. One about furniture repair and refinishing that was stained with varnish splashes had belonged to Taggert L. Mickelson. Mark remembered Mr. Mickelson, who had once lived in the house down the road.

Since all the books in two boxes seemed to go together, Mark combined them into one carton. "Are there two *l*'s in *college*?" he asked Kelli, who watched him letter a sign for the box. In red felt marker it read: SAVE $30,475! COMPLETE COLLEGE EDUCATION—SPECIAL: $10.

"Mark, nobody can save thirty thousand, four hundred seventy-five dollars at a garage sale. That's ridiculous." One by one Kelli looked at the titles: *History of Western Civilization, Poetry of the Romantic Period, Biology, General Economics, Art Through the Ages, American Government.*

"See, they're all here." Mark pointed to a name on an inside cover. "All the books this girl had at college. Here's the name of her dorm. A person buys these for ten dollars, takes them home, and reads them. He's saved himself thirty thousand, four hundred and seventy-five dollars. College costs thirty thousand, four hundred eighty-five dollars."

Kelli slapped the books down one on top of the other. "How do you know?"

"Saw it on *Sixty Minutes*," Mark said with assurance. He picked up a slim blue paperback with a sketch of a rolled-up document on the cover. The title was on the ribbon flowing from around the scroll. "*GED*," he read, " 'general education diploma, an *a-c-h-i-e-v*—' "

"Achievable," Kelli pronounced for him.

He leafed through the booklet. "So here's one for you, Kelli. How to get the high school diploma you want. You can have this book free."

"Let me see that." She read as she went inside.

Scott grabbed the felt pen right out of Mark's hand. "I'll make us some signs. We won't need many with all the traffic already on Hardin Road."

Scott's cramped scrawl was terrible. He wrote as if his fingers were broken. "Maybe Mom would make us some signs in her fancy script," Mark suggested.

"Nobody can read that old-fashioned kind of writing. This is a modern, up-to-date sale." Scott messed up two more pieces of cardboard. His signs sure weren't eye-catching.

In Mark's opinion, nothing looked as homemade as a

homemade sign. He had a much better idea for advertising the sale, but he kept it to himself.

Mark had to watch his step. Scott would walk off the job if he thought his little brother was too bossy. When Scott priced the sickening light at two dollars, Mark didn't say a word. Later he had a chance to change the mark to thirty-five cents. Every sale should have some great bargains.

Mark cleared a space around the set of weights. Then he took the *Encyclopedia of Sports* from where he had put it,behind the burned-out slow cooker. "Hey, look at this." He looked through the book as if he'd just discovered it. "Everything is here. Sure enough, weight lifting here in the back. Let's take a break from this junk, Scott. If I have to lick both Skinners with one hand tied behind my back, I'll have to work out."

Scott looked at the diagrams. "Nothing much to it except starting light, working up, practice." He slid disks marked "2½ kg" on the barbell. Mark liked the way the collars slid smoothly along the bar to lock the disks in place.

"A baby could lift this." Scott brought the bar to his shoulders. As he lifted it over his head, he bumped a garage rafter. Empty cartons stored on it came tumbling down.

Mark jumped aside as the barbell came down suddenly. "Wasn't that a little too fast, Scott?"

"There's not enough room to lift, let alone control," Scott complained.

Mark consulted the sports book. "Clean. That's a lift that only goes to the shoulders. You can do that one."

"Okay. I'll try the ten kilograms." He slipped more weights on the bar.

"How much is a kilogram?" Mark asked. "I don't think we've had that yet in school."

"It's a thousand grams. Easy to remember."

"I mean, how much is it really?" Mark locked the collars around the bar.

"About two point two pounds. Get with it, Mark. Think metric. You sure have a lot to learn."

"I know," Mark agreed. "Now try the clean lift. It says right here that you're supposed to bring it up with one movement without any violent contact with your body."

With three jerky movements and a hard knee bump Scott lifted the barbell. Then it came down, fast, with a thud.

"I'd call that pretty violent," Mark said. "Better try it again." He encouraged Scott to practice the clean lift ten more times before Scott lightened the weights and told Mark it was his turn.

Mark felt nauseated and saw red spots before his eyes from the strain of two lifts. He was glad when Mom came out and said she was telling Scott for the last time to come in and do his exercises.

* * *

At the Wilderness Area the next morning Mark's only damage was mud all over the back of his jacket from Jack's tripping him into a puddle. The bus came before the Skinners had time to search him and find the heavy stapler in his jacket pocket.

After school he was able to brush most of the dry dirt off his jacket so he wouldn't get the car seat dirty when he got a ride to Hardin Grove. A classmate's mother was driving him to the orthodontist, so she agreed to take Mark right to the *Hardin Grove Herald*.

A woman who looked kind of gray, like a wet newspaper, was the only person in the cramped front office of the *Herald*. Mark asked her for some printed garage sale signs.

The fluorescent orange signs she put on the counter brightened the dingy office. She moved to her typewriter. "Now how do you want the ad worded?"

"I just want the signs. No ads." With his heavy-tip pen Mark started to fill in the blank spaces on a sign for the time and place of his sale.

She took back the bright squares. "We give these only when ads are run." She leaned across to Mark as if letting him in on a secret. "Classifieds are your best buy. Low rates for two insertions in good positions. Garage freaks read them all. Here, write it out." She handed him a piece of newsprint. "Time, place, your best items."

She spread back pages of the *Herald* on the counter. "This morning's ads will give you some ideas."

After a little study Mark wrote: "Super garage sale, Sat., March 25, 9:00 A.M. to 4:00 P.M., valuable books, toys, crafts, small appliances, novelty lamp, many bargains, luggage."

As he tried to think of how to list the rest of the accumulation, he looked beyond the business office into the newsroom. It was as drab as the office of his school principal, who at least had a potted snake plant.

A pretty young woman in a red blouse pushed her long hair back from her face as she read yards of paper coming out of a ticking machine. Others in the big room strolled or rushed around, talked on phones, typed, smoked, stared into space, and paid no attention to one another. Each one seemed to be working alone. Mark wondered how they put a whole newspaper together, but they did, every day.

The Zanzutus didn't even have paper, let alone a printed newspaper. They had runners who went from village to village when something really weird happened, such as the sudden appearance of a kid speaking a strange language. To train as a Zanzutu runner was a great honor. Boys about Mark's age were selected.

Still, he thought he'd have to teach the Zanzutus to make paper since it was really handy stuff. Wasps could make paper. They had hardly any brains at all in their little nailheads. He should be able to do at least as well.

"You'd better finish if you want that in tomorrow." The woman looked at Mark's ad. "How about collectibles?" Mark asked how to spell the word and added it. "Any antiques?" she asked.

Mark nodded. Those boxes from Mrs. McSwiggen were doubtless full of antiques, besides the Fryes' old stuff.

"Better put antiques first; they're always a draw."

Mark crossed out and rewrote the beginning. He needed a snappy ending and glanced over published ads for ideas. Some were run by churches and charities. He thought of his and Scott's need to pay for the weight set. Mark added: "Support Worthy Youth Fitness Program, get bargains, have fun."

The gray lady nodded her approval as she read his ad, so he knew he'd written a good one. People would be all over their yard, crowded around the garage, under the pine tree.

"Wait a second." Mark took his ad back and added: "Not responsible for accidents."

She handed him a fistful of orange signs. "Now who gets the bill? I'll need name, address, and telephone number of the treasurer of this worthy youth fitness organization."

Mark elected himself to office on the spot and gave her the information. He filled in the blanks on the signs and set out to post them at intersections and other good places. His handy stapler made fast work of putting up the notices, and Mark pretended to be a Zanzutu runner between postings.

Lately Scott hadn't cared whether Mark came or went. Now he was actually waiting anxiously for him at home. "Wow! Are you late! Where have you been?"

"Putting up our signs."

Scott slid weights on the bar. "I was wondering where my signs had gone."

Mark didn't tell him those awful homemade signs had gone under the living-room rug.

CHAPTER SEVEN

Skunk cabbage leaves were unrolling in the Wilderness Area swamp, and long, pollen-dusted tassels decorated the gray birch trees by the bus shelter. On Friday morning spring had put the Skinners in a frolicsome mood. They merely snatched Mark's cap, played catch with it, then threw it on top of the shelter just as the bus appeared. Mark didn't want to be up there retrieving his cap when the bus stopped. He let it go; it was a winter cap anyhow.

When they arrived at school, La Vern grabbed Mark around the waist, pinning his arms to his sides. Despite his weight lifting, Mark didn't have the muscle to break free. From his book bag Jack produced two of Mark's signs, tore them up, and tossed the pieces in his face.

He didn't know how many more they had destroyed, but he hoped enough remained to spread the word. After school he checked the morning *Herald* and knew that his ads would surely help.

At bedtime that evening Mark lay awake a long time listening to the spring peeper frogs. He woke several times during the night. At six o'clock he got up and dressed. It was daylight, and no more sleep was possible. Then he woke Scott, who had promised to help at least until they had taken in enough to pay for the weights.

Mark was glad Kelli wouldn't be around. She had a full shift at Charley's Chicken. Mom left early for exercise class, which was before the career conference.

Mark's excitement grew with each car and pickup that stopped. He knew most of the people who milled around the yard, but he was firm. No sales until nine A.M.

Some women clustered at the garage windows, trying to see what was inside. A neatly dressed man had a tape line and carefully measured all the used clothing in one of Mrs. McSwiggen's boxes that was outside. A kid wanted to buy Ozro, who was shut up in his run so he wouldn't jump on the paying customers.

A ragged line was forming at the garage door when a beat-up black panel truck with a blue fender rattled up the driveway. A monster of a man got out and tried to hitch up his pants. He wore a greasy wool cap too small for his big head. His dirty T-shirt was too short to cover a strip of his fat belly, which was also dirty. He pushed in at the head of the line.

"Who's runnin' this nickel-and-dime show?" he boomed out.

Mark overheard himself described by someone as the blond kid with the big ears.

"Hey, boy," the big fellow shouted at Mark, "you'd better get this show open before you lose your crowd." He kicked at the garage door.

Mark was relieved when Scott finally appeared and set up a card table for checkout. He had a yellow candy box ready for cash.

At one minute after nine o'clock the young woman with a baby in a stroller was at Scott's table with three of Kelli's stuffed animals and a potty chair, which Mom had decided not to keep for her grandchildren. The man with the tape measure was next with an armful of trousers and shirts. A lady babbled about how happy she was to find plastic plates and dented saucepans for her son's apartment. Dad's fishing rod, which he no longer had time to use, went right away. A woman who said she was into recycling country crafts was pleased with an old quilt with some of the stuffing coming out. Another buyer took all the wooden picture frames but left the plastic ones.

In all the grabbing Mark didn't have time to feel too bad when a careless-looking kid carried away his old road-building toys.

The sign on the college books was knocked down twice before a spry old gentleman took the lot. "Never could resist a bargain," he said as Mark helped him carry the books to his car. "This is my last chance for a college education. Besides I'm helping this youth program. Might be tax-deductible."

A lot of people mentioned the worthy cause. Scott looked puzzled and embarrassed when complimented for his unselfish project for others. Mark kept away from the checkout table so Scott couldn't ask him for an explanation. He bagged purchases, straightened stacks of books, hunted requested items, quoted prices, and kept little kids out of the road.

He noticed two women going into the house and ran to tell them that nothing in there was for sale. They said they knew but just loved to see other people's homes.

Mark had to take back Kelli's good set of battery jumpers from a teenager, who also wanted to buy Scott's Honda. He hurried to return the jumpers to the garage just as the huge man came crashing out from the barricaded back area marked: PRIVATE, DO NOT ENTER. NOTHING FOR SALE.

"How much for that wrecked pink desk back there?" he demanded. "No price, but I put my 'sold' sticker on it. We can negotiate."

"I don't think I ought to sell that," Mark said. "We keep my dog's food in the drawers."

"No use storing it away. I pay good prices; you'd be surprised. It's taking up a lot of good room."

Mark was unsure. "I don't know. My mom's away

today, so I can't ask her. It's just me and my big brother, and I guess he'll take off after a while."

The man pulled a wadded bit of paper out of his pocket. "Your ad says antiques. I don't see none."

"Well, just any of this stuff." Mark waved his arm over the dwindled stock.

The big man scowled and snorted. "Lotta junk. I shoulda kept on goin' when I saw it wasn't at the old lady's the way I expected." He jerked his fat head toward Mrs. McSwiggen's.

Mark was glad to see his broad back as he went toward his truck, but he turned around again. His scowl was replaced by a gap-toothed grin. "It's a good one on me. Ya see from the address I figured the sale was at her place. I know she's a collector, and I heard she's got to sell out."

He picked up the floating-glob light. "Well, since I'm here, might as well get something. I'll give you a couple of bucks for this." Mark thought he hadn't seen the thirty-five-cent price sticker under his dirty thumb. "And you boys have this marked way too low." He put the dinner-roll warmer under his arm. "I'll give you a dollar fifty more for it. Might as well throw in this busted stool you've got at a dollar. I'll give you three. One leg cracked, one gone. I might be able to fix it."

He waddled off to the checkout table and waited patiently behind a woman and her three small children. The mother had bags of knickknacks, and the kids clutched the last of Kelli's stuffed animals. The big fellow paid the high prices and gave the boys a big wave when he drove away.

"Santa Claus without a suit." Scott thumped his table.

"At first he was mean," Mark said. "But I guess his heart is as big as the rest of him."

"Either that or he's just plain ignorant. He pays more than things are worth." Scott shook his head. "It takes all kinds. It was a good thing I was here when they all came at once. Just stragglers now."

"Sure. Your experienced garage sale freaks read all the ads and come early and skim off the cream." Mark looked at the sad stock of leavings. "Nothing now but low-fat milk."

Mark wanted to count the money in the cashbox but decided that would look greedy in front of customers. There were only two now. He did take a peek into the box and drew a quick breath.

As he waited for the woman to finish browsing, he wondered what the Zanzutus used for money. Maybe they had shells or polished stones instead of coins. He wasn't sure he could persuade them that paper money was valuable. That would be especially hard since he himself didn't understand why. Still, he was happy to glimpse a stack of it in the box.

He decided to reduce prices and went to tell the couple still looking of their great luck. The man shook his head. "Nothing here I can't live without. Let's go," he urged his wife. "We've got a houseful. You don't need anything else."

"I know I don't need anything," she agreed, "but I can still *want* something." She seemed disappointed not to have found it when they finally left.

Scott counted the bills, and Mark counted the change. The total was forty-three dollars and forty-five cents. Mark was elated.

"Not too bad." Scott straightened a stack of coins. "Plenty to pay your senior citizen pal for her weights and her other stuff. Are you sure a nice old lady like Mrs. McSwiggen won't give you the weights?"

"She's got this cash-flow problem," Mark said.

Scott put some bills aside. "Here's twenty dollars. I checked in the Sears catalog. That ought to do it for used weights."

"Right. Old Dirty Belly—you know, that big guy that paid too much—helped pay for them. After we pay Mrs. McSwiggen, we'll have around twenty-three whole dollars left." Mark paused. "I'll need a little of that to pay for our ads."

"What ads?"

It occurred to Mark that everyone had been too busy that morning to look at the *Herald*. He brought the newspaper to the checkout table, spread it open, and pointed to two places. "There they are in black and white. Two insertions yesterday, two this morning. They sure brought the crowd. We got good signs too, free."

"Free! I'll bet." Scott read the ad. "Nobody told you to put this in. How much was it?"

"I don't know exactly."

"Well, I'll tell you exactly. The want ad rates are here in black and white, too." Scott counted lines and figured on the newspaper margin. "Exactly twenty-seven dollars and forty cents. And what's this 'Worthy Youth Fitness Program'? Is that why people were talking about a good cause?"

"Could be," Mark admitted. "It is a sort of fitness program. I have to get in shape to lick the Skinners, and you—" Mark stopped without telling Scott the lifting sessions were also to help his back.

"Two of us fooling around with weights is not a Worthy Youth Fitness Program spelled in capital letters. You can get in trouble printing lies like that."

"What kind of trouble?"

"So now you ask me!" Scott shouted. "After you've run up a big bill. You didn't ask me about anything first. You never talk things over."

Mark signaled him to lower his voice. An elderly man wearing a checked flannel shirt and a fluorescent orange hunting cap walked stiffly toward the sale leftovers. At first Mark didn't recognize Taggert L. Mickelson. He was thinner and more stooped than he had been when he lived in the neighborhood.

"Mark, isn't it?" he said in a high, husky voice. He flicked Mark's ear with his big fingers. "I remember you, even if you have changed considerably." Mark could have said the same about Mr. Mickelson, but he didn't.

Scott stumbled on the table leg as he stood up. Mr. Mickelson looked him up and down. "How's the weather up there, Scott? I'll bet you've grown a foot."

"So I've heard. What am I supposed to do about it?" Scott stamped over to the pine tree and climbed up.

Mr. Mickelson cocked his head in surprise. "He's a mite touchy, I'd say."

"Maybe because it's getting near lunchtime," Mark offered as explanation.

"Yes, and I suppose your best items are gone." He looked at scattered curlers, tangled balls of yarn, buckets of dried paint. "First thing this morning I had to take in the flea market. It's a big one, spilling out of the fire hall."

Mark told him of all the good things he had missed. "We sold a book that had belonged to you. It had your name in it. It was about refinishing furniture."

"Came back to the old neighborhood, same as I did. I sold all my books when I left Hardin Grove awhile back."

"I remember that. You were going to drive all over the country all the time. I thought that was neat." Mark looked toward the road. "Where's your camper?"

"Traded her in on a mobile home over on Westline Road." Mr. Mickelson told Mark that endless recreation in his vehicle hadn't been as carefree as he had expected.

He searched for a place to stop and paid high fees to hook up to utilities and to dump his waste. Police in some towns wouldn't let him park his housekeeping rig overnight. He got tired of traveling and came back to Hardin Grove.

"So if my book comes around again, grab it for me." He showed Mark his stained fingernails. "I'm refinishing furniture again. Come by my place, and I'll show you the shop I've built onto my mobile home. I picked up a couple of pieces at the flea market today. I'll soon have them looking first-class."

"How was Mrs. McSwiggen doing at the flea market?"

"All right on the selling." Mr. Mickelson shook his head. "Otherwise, she's not doing too good. Claims she might be moving. She didn't tell me why, so I didn't ask."

After Mr. Mickelson had left, Mark called up to Scott. "We made twenty-five more cents. He took that wire corn popper. So come on down. We'll get some milk and peanut butter and jelly sandwiches. Then we can work out with the weights."

Scott dropped down. "There's not enough room to do anything around here. If we lift in our room, we'll knock a hole in the ceiling. Give them back to Mrs. McSwiggen." He took some money out of the cashbox. "I'm going to the pizza place to get myself something to eat. I've had enough of your supersale."

"Scott, you'd better stay here and help me sell the rest of this stuff. We're three dollars and seventy cents in the hole."

"Where do you get that *we* business? It's your problem." Scott turned his back on Mark, hunched over, and walked away.

CHAPTER EIGHT

ark was too discouraged to recount the cash. The game arcade was next to the pizzeria. Scott had probably helped himself to more than food funds. A peanut butter and jelly sandwich didn't make Mark feel much better. If Mrs. McSwiggen had been home, she doubtless would have brought him a plate of warm sugar cookies and stayed to keep him company. He didn't want to roll those weights back to her house. She needed that sale.

Mark watched every approaching car. They all whizzed by. Maybe he wouldn't sell another thing. He felt as desolate as Ozro sounded howling in his dog run by the back fence. With no one around there was no reason to keep him fastened.

Ozro jumped for joy to be loose. Eagerly he sniffed

and dug among the dry weed stalks as if catching up on neglected work. Zanzutu dogs were born hunters and roamed freely over Zanzutu country, which wasn't cut up into little pieces like a pan of pudding.

Mark imagined the area around him as one vast tract— the Frye yard; Mrs. McSwiggen's place; the brushy, overgrown field behind his house; land for the new mall; the Skinners' land; the Wilderness Area. With a dry weed for his poison-tipped dart he crouched low and followed Ozro, who was on the trail of a vicious wild boar.

He heard mocking laughter. Jack and La Vern pranced and hooted by the garage.

"Sic 'em Ozro," Mark hissed. Ozro charged toward the Skinners, hackles down, tail wagging. Jack grabbed one of Mrs. McSwiggen's boxes. La Vern shouldered a bulging bag.

They ran from the yard, then stopped to examine their loot. Jack dropped the box labeled: CLEAN RAGS. "Junk. Lousy old junk," he yelled.

La Vern's bag of wire hangers rattled as he threw it down. "Yeah. Keep your old junk."

Mark wished they had kept going with their stolen goods. He didn't know what he would do with it, and Mom wouldn't want her rummage dragged back into the house. For two more hours he'd have to sit around and look at things still cluttering the garage.

He felt drowsy and squirmed in the upholstered chair with broken springs until he was comfortable. Ozro pawed a carpet scrap, turned around and around, then curled up at his feet. They both napped.

The roar of a muffler with a hole in it roused Mark. The black panel truck came up the drive. "I'm back," Dirty Belly said as he got out. "I got to thinking to myself. Now there's them boys doing something for our youth, and they're going to have a lot of odds and ends left. So I've come back to help you." He looked around. "Where's your brother, the tall guy?"

When he learned that Scott wasn't around, he said it didn't matter. He and Mark could do business. He considered the remainders on the long table and around the garage. "Not too much left. I'd be able to go thirty dollars for all of it. I'll haul it away for you. Leave everything clean as a whistle."

"You will?" Mark could hardly believe his luck.

"Now by rights you can't close up until four o'clock. I've got nearly a full load on now, so I'll go empty my truck and be back around a quarter of four."

He was in no hurry to go. With his big belly as a bumper he pushed around an outdoor grill and a coil of garden hose to the old desk in the rear of the garage. "You still won't have room to swing a cat back here. The best place for dog food is right in the bag. Keeps it fresher." He left more fingerprints on the front of a desk drawer when he popped open a paint blister to show bare wood. With a finger moistened in his mouth he rubbed the bare spot.

Bits of pink paint were already chipped off the sides of the desk and showed dark wood. Canned dog food that Mom had bought on special sale was stacked on the desktop and on the shelf above it. Dirty Belly raised the quarter cylinder that came down over the writing space of the desk. Mark had always liked this neat cover, but the pigeonholes inside weren't large enough to store much of anything. Dirty Belly could get only two fat fingers into the hand grooves to pull out the writing board. The board didn't slide back smoothly. He rubbed his big paws over the paint-clogged fan carvings decorating the three lower drawers and examined the joints of each as he pulled it out. A drawer full of dry dog food jammed and stuck when he tried to close it.

"It's in awful shape. Needs a lot of work. But I'll give you fifteen dollars for it."

Mark tried to hide his satisfaction at the offer. Dirty Belly paid too much for everything, so fifteen dollars must be more than the desk was worth. Besides, Mark was grateful to him for buying the leftovers. If Mark made this sale, Scott wouldn't be mad at him about the ad. He looked around for someplace to put Ozro's food.

"Well, all right. Seventeen-fifty. That's the best I can do. Here it is. Cash." He counted greasy bills and a coin into Mark's hand. "I just might have enough room to get it in my truck right now." He spilled two days' ration of dog food on the floor as he dumped pellets from the drawer into a bushel basket.

Mark tried to help him lift the leadlike desk, but Dirty Belly said he could get it on his back and carry it alone if Mark would clear a path for him. In no time he had it loaded and tied in his truck. Now he was in a hurry to leave.

Somehow thinking of such a helpful person only as Dirty Belly didn't seem right. "What's your name?" Mark asked.

He leaned out the truck window to give Mark his big, gap-toothed grin. "Some folks call me the Generous Gent."

"Okay, Generous Gent. See you at quarter of four," Mark yelled to be heard over the racing motor and roaring muffler. The panel truck careened down the drive and into Hardin Road without stopping.

Mark jumped around the cleared space in the garage. Scott was sure to appreciate all the weight-lifting room. He took a stance and went through the motions of bringing a weight bar smoothly to his shoulders. Quickly he brought it up with arms outstretched over his head. He could easily do the clean and jerk lift, but he knew Scott couldn't with the rafters overhead.

Of course, there was the outdoors for practicing, Mark thought as he went across the yard to the side door to see the kitchen clock. But surprise was a big part of his strategy against the Skinners. Besides, Scott might balk at working out before everybody passing on Hardin Road. Inside, where they could lift in privacy—every day, rain or shine—would be better.

As he carried the barbell to the cleared area, he knocked Dad's handsaw down from a nail on the garage wall. Mark studied the pattern of rafters overhead. There sure were a lot of them. If he sawed out a part of just one rafter between a roof truss, there would be plenty of room for Scott's overhead lifts.

Sawing from a stepladder wasn't so easy. Once into the two-by-four rafter, the saw bowed unless he glided it just right. Mark was anxious to finish the job by a quarter of four. Finally the saw whined through the last splinter of the second cut. The section of rafter clunked to the floor.

Mark folded the stepladder, leaned it against a bag of charcoal, and shoved the cut rafter under it. He checked the time again and was glad to see that it was twenty minutes until four. Something was coming, but it wasn't noisy enough to be the panel truck. He knew the sound of their old car.

"Sixty-one dollars and twenty cents. That's what we took in so far, and more's coming," Mark shouted to Mom as she got out of the car with a bag of groceries. "All the rest of this is going to be cleared out of here in a minute."

Mom was delighted. She'd had no idea the accumulation would bring so much.

"Where's Scott?" she asked. "Did he do his exercises today?"

"Day's not over." Mark glanced toward the road. "It's not even four o'clock." He dug into a package of cookies from the grocery bag he carried into the kitchen, where he continued his report on the day. "And there was this big guy, Mom, the Generous Gent. I think he must do some kind of rough, dirty work. He's coming back; you'll get to see him."

"I want to hear all about it a little later, Mark." Mom hurried to sort groceries on the kitchen counter. "Now I've got to do some straightening up and get dinner planned for Dad, and I can't understand a word you're saying with your mouth full."

Scott didn't say anything to Mark or Mom when he came home. He kept stuffing cookies into his mouth until the package was empty. Mark could hardly wait to see Scott's surprise when the Generous Gent showed up and handed over thirty dollars. Mark stood by the door so he could see him arrive. It was ten minutes after four.

Mark couldn't keep all the good news to himself. He drummed on the lid of the candy box. "Scott, I took in seventeen dollars and fifty cents after you left."

Scott tore open a package of pretzels. "I'll bet."

"Well, I did," Mark insisted.

"You did not. There's as much junk out there as when I left."

"I did so," Mark shouted. "Sold a high-ticket item."

"Like what?" Scott demanded.

"Now don't you boys start squabbling." Mom was looking for a place to conceal a bag of potato chips. "Scott, take your cap off in the house and go do your exercises."

Scott didn't move. "In this family I'm pushed around like a shopping cart. You don't have to tell me when to do everything."

"I'm telling you now for the last time. You know Dr. Feluchi said every day without fail. We want to have a good report for Dad."

"We!" Scott groaned.

Mark started to follow him into the living room, where he could see Hardin Road from the front window.

"Just a minute, Mark." Mom held his shoulder. "I've got a dozen things to do at once, but before Dad comes, I've got a bone to pick with you. I ran into your swimming teacher at the supermarket. He said he had considered you a challenge." Mom widened her eyes in surprise. "He's sorry you dropped his class."

"Dropped his class! I didn't know anybody was allowed to do that, so how could I . . . wait, Mom, somebody's stopping out front."

Mark dashed out hoping to escape Mom's questions and to greet the Generous Gent. But it was Kelli who was there waving good-bye to a fellow who had given her a ride home. Mark reported the success of the sale to her and asked if she'd passed a black panel truck with a blue fender.

She shook her head. "Wasn't looking for one either." Her voice sounded as if she had a cold. An allergy was plenty stubborn. Kelli would surely thank him when hers ended.

She riffled through a McSwiggen box. "You've got a lot of depressing stuff left, Mark, but you did swell, considering the silly sale season has started. A lot of people are pulling things out of the house and piling them in the yards to sell. There were some women in Charley's Chicken talking about how much fun they'd had browsing today at all the sales. Another big guy was bragging to them about a desk he got for a song. Must be a special antique from the way he described it. An Eastlake cylinder-front desk, he called it."

Mark felt as jolted as a bird flying into a picture window. "What did he look like, that big guy?"

"Looked like a piano mover." Kelli started inside. "Mom, how was the career conference? Say, what's an Eastlake cylinder-front desk?" Mark heard her ask before she closed the door.

As Mark watched the road and listened, he tried to calm his churning stomach. All kinds of people, all sizes, bought and sold old desks every day. Seventeen dollars and fifty cents wasn't a song. It was hard cash. Besides, nobody would paint a genuine valuable antique desk pink.

All the passing cars purred by quietly. Maybe the panel truck had broken down, lost its muffler.

Robins called as they flew low over the yard. Frogs began to peep in the Wilderness Area. Thunder rumbled as clouds rolled across the low sun. Ozro, who was fearful of thunder, huddled and whined by the side door. Mark opened it just enough to let him inside. Mark wished he could slip in, too. He was lonely and beginning to feel hungry, but he dreaded to go into his own house.

CHAPTER NINE

Rolling spurts of a powerful diesel engine echoed down Hardin Road. Two sets of headlights and top cab lights outlined the big rig that was skillfully maneuvered into the driveway. Air brakes hissed and sighed. Wheeler Frye, independent trucker, was home.

Dad's arms were full, but he managed to tousle Mark's hair as they hurried inside just ahead of the rain. The house always seemed smaller when Dad was home. He flung a pair of boots in a corner and tossed two jackets and a duffel bag on the kitchen counter. He hugged Mom and kissed her with a big smack. She couldn't hug him back with meat loaf mixings on her hands.

Dad bent forward, then straightened up. "I've got an awful case of interstate back. How's everything here at Eighteen-ten Hardin Road?"

"Well, we're still kickin'. Some of us could kick harder." Mom looked knowingly at Mark. First thing, Mom was ready to tell Dad he was a swimming-class drop-out.

Mark rattled the cashbox. "Dad, we had this big sale today. We're rich."

Mom patted the meat into a loaf and put it in the oven. "Mark went into business and did well, too. The other kids are here somewhere, laying low, so they won't have to help me."

Dad threw back his head and hollered. "Kelli, Scott, I'm home."

"I hate to tell you, Wheeler." Mom spoke in a low voice. "Scott's back is no better. You've got to talk turkey with him about doing those exercises. He's so surly with me. You'd think I wasn't on his side."

Scott came and said hello in a wobbly up-and-down voice as if Dad were nobody special. He slumped in a kitchen chair instead of starting to roughhouse with Dad the way he used to do.

Kelli gave Dad a happy greeting, but she looked sad. "What's the matter, hon? You been crying?"

She tried to smile as she wiped her eyes. "No, maybe it's tree bud pollen, something. No telling what."

"How's the old Chrysler?"

"Hurtin'. I think the reverse gear has slipped off the shift forks. I've got to fix it. Lots of things I want to do."

Mom put potatoes in beside the meat loaf. "Right now you can set the table."

"I haven't got time, Mom. I've got to take my uniforms out of the dryer before they get wrinkled."

"All I get are excuses." Mom whomped a head of lettuce on the counter to loosen the core. "Well, dinner's going to be a little late. With everything to do, no help, I didn't get the meat loaf in as soon as planned."

"I put in a shift at Charley's Chicken, and that's no fun," Kelli said.

"I've been thinking all day about a good home-cooked meal. Truck stop food is ruining my stomach." Dad took a roll of antacid tablets from his shirt pocket and put two in his mouth. "I'm living on these things and coffee."

Kelli climbed over Scott's long legs, which blocked her way out of the kitchen. "How about Big Foot here being helpful? Once he delivers the Sunday newspapers, he just lolls around the rest of the week. Doesn't do anything around here anymore. Not even his exercises."

Scott's heavy brows frowned into a straight line. "So I'll set the table. No big thing." He took five plates from the cupboard. "I hope we have something on this table besides dishes. I'm famished." He glided plates across the table as if he were dealing cards. One slid off the edge and crashed into pieces on the floor.

Mom put her fists to the sides of her head and firmed her mouth in a straight line. She was trying hard to control her temper. "Just let it go, Scott," she said as she got the broom. "This kind of help I don't need."

Dad looked up at Scott. "I think you've put another inch on top. Now, what's this I hear about your not doing those exercises?"

Scott shrugged. "Mom's gone a lot. Sometimes she's not here when I do them. It sure is no fun doing those dumb exercises."

"Fun!" Dad boomed. "It seems I'm hearing an awful lot about fun. Since when did everything have to be fun? Do you think it's fun behind the wheel hour after hour, staring at that white line, getting so stiff you can hardly climb down from the cab when you stop? You wonder when the next crazy driver will cut in too close or if the brakes will hold on a two-mile downhill pitch, what you'll do if they fail. For real fun you can think about the price of gas and the truck payments. I don't want to hear any more about fun."

Without a word Kelli fled to her room. Scott grabbed his cap and slammed the door as he went out into the rain.

Mom patted Dad's shoulder. "They didn't mean anything. Kids just naturally complain. I'm hoping to find something I can work into that will be a real help for us. I keep trying different things. I guess I keep hoping I'll have a little fun along with it." Mom almost cried when she mentioned fun. "It's hard for me, too, Wheeler, with you on the road all the time. Sometimes I get tired of being cheerleader." Mom sniffed and blinked back tears. "This isn't what I expected this evening to be."

It wasn't what Mark had expected either. He had to face facts. Dirty Belly wasn't coming back. Nobody ever called him the Generous Gent. Dirty Belly was a big fat liar.

Shouts and yelps came from Kelli's room. Ozro thumped down the hall and slid across the kitchen linoleum. Kelli was after him with a baton of rolled newspaper.

Mom shoved Ozro out. "Mark, I'm telling you for the last time, keep that big yellow mutt out of the house. In Kelli's room, of all places."

"It was thundering, and he was scared." Mark's explanation was ignored.

Kelli narrowed her eyes. "I went to hang up my uniforms. There he was in the back of my closet. And that's not all. My stuffed animals are gone."

Mark tried to sound cheerful. "So you had a real live dog there instead of dirty toy ones stuffed with unknown fibers that were probably—"

Kelli was too angry to listen. "I'm not kiddin', Mark. You sold them at your cruddy garage sale, didn't you? Didn't ask anybody. Just did it."

Mark opened the cashbox. "How much were they worth?"

"Priceless," she declared, "and you can just get them back."

Dad took another tablet from his roll. "It's lonesome on the road, but in some ways more peaceful."

Mom's long, forlorn face surrounded by her curly permanent was like a picture in the wrong frame. If Mom was glum, the whole family would stay out of sorts. She hadn't tossed the salad. They might never have dinner.

"I'll give you more work space here, Linda." Dad picked up from the counter a ten-pound bag of dog food Mom had bought on special sale. Mark sure wished the old desk were still in the garage for him to put it in.

He'd have to tell Mom. Mark smoothed the bills he took from the cashbox so she'd see they weren't ones. "This is for you, for that old desk. This huge guy really paid big prices."

Mom stared at Mark in disbelief. "My desk! You didn't sell my antique desk!" She leaned against the counter for support. "My great-great-grandfather *made* that desk."

Things were even worse than Mark had feared. "It was in the garage painted pink," he said feebly.

Mom didn't want money either. She wanted her desk back. That very day she had paid for a course at the Y in furniture refinishing. The desk had been in her room when she was growing up. She was twelve years old when she slapped a coat of paint over the dark walnut burl-trimmed wood. She had painted all her furniture pink. For a long time she'd been meaning to refinish her desk. Her voice faltered as she started to tell how her great-great-grandfather had made it.

Suddenly there was a crash, curses, and groans from the garage. Then Dad came in and stood silently. Raindrops glistened on his bald head. One fist was clenched.

He made a real effort to speak calmly. "In some ways it's safer out on the road. I was trying to get to the light switch. Down comes the saw. Could have ripped off a finger. Then I got the stepladder right across my back." He opened his hand to show fresh sawdust. His voice rose. "I want to know who the Sam Hill cut a good weight-bearing rafter."

Much later they had dried-out meat loaf and scorched potatoes for dinner. Mark was ordered to remain at the table even though he had no appetite. Mom didn't apologize for the food or for the lack of dessert. She seemed more sad than mad. Dad ended his meal with two stomach tablets and three cups of coffee.

CHAPTER TEN

The rain had stopped by the time Mark escaped outdoors to sit on the dry top step of the front porch. Ozro sniffed him out and was all over him like a fur snowsuit. He acted as if nothing miserable had happened.

"What's wrong with you, Ozro? My whole family is mad at me. Aren't you going to bite me or something?" Ozro crowded close to Mark and, for the first time, stuck out his paw in the handshake trick Mark had tried so hard to teach him. "Ozro, it's too bad you're not a retriever. We've got to get some things back from our sale." Mark put his head down on Ozro's damp coat. "You know something, Ozro? You smell like a wet dog."

In the light from the front picture window Mark tried to pick burdock stickers from Ozro's matted fur. Since the weed seeds were the same color as Ozro, they were hard to see.

He could see easily enough that a family discussion was going on in the living room. Mark was certain he was the subject. Scott stood in the middle of the floor, spilling the beans about something. Then he grabbed his cap and hurried out of the room. From all the headshaking he must have told how much the ad for the sale had cost. Yes—Mom located the *Herald* to see for herself in black and white that their sale was to benefit a made-up youth program.

A flashlight beam shone on Ozro. Scott's voice came from the gloom. "Just checked my Honda to see if you sold anything off it. It's not a parts bike, and don't you forget it." He held the light closer. "Sawing a good rafter. Why did you do a fool thing like that without asking anybody?"

Mark kept on picking burs. If Scott had bothered to listen to his explanation, he'd probably claim Mark was trying to put part of the blame on him. Mark didn't want to hear any more about the rafter, so he changed the subject. "Jack and La Vern Skinner came and took some stuff from our sale."

"And what did you do about it?"

Ozro yelped as Mark pulled both his fur and a bur. "Nothin'. How can I defend myself or our property unless you help me get in shape?"

Scott shone the light on the garage. "It's done now,

and the roof won't fall in until the snow comes again. There's a little more room in back, so we might as well work out with the weights."

They lifted, not only that evening but also every day of the following week, which was spring vacation at both their schools. Better still, it was a blessed vacation from bus-stop abuse.

Mark danced around like a referee and barked orders like a tough coach as Scott strained under increasing weight. "All right. A little smoother this time. Use your hook grip for the clean and jerk. Split as you lift, and don't lower the bar until I signal."

Scott gritted his teeth and lifted the barbell to his shoulders. As he stood erect, he jerked the bar up through the opening of the severed rafter. His face contorted, and cords stood out in his neck as he held the bar over his head with arms locked. Mark could just feel those back muscles strengthening. As long as he dared, he held off his signal. Then he clapped his hands and jumped aside in case the weight crashed down.

Being Scott's coach was great compared with the pain of lifting. Still, Mark took his turn every day and worked out until his arms felt like spaghetti. However, for some odd reason he was not getting stronger.

He'd have been lonely without the workouts with Scott. The house seemed empty after Dad had left. Mom dropped her course in furniture refinishing and started her master class in cake decorating. When Mark tried to chat with Kelli, she was busy and sent him out of her room. But he noticed she was studying the book on general education diplomas that he'd given her from the sale. She took it to work with her in case there was a lull.

Mark wished he could get rid of the sale leftovers the Zanzutu way; the Zanzutu Burning Festival coincided with school spring vacation. Some of the sale debris was too soggy to burn; besides, if he started a bonfire, the township cops and volunteer fire fighters would be there with sirens screaming. Finally, Mom made him take money from the cashbox to pay a disposal company to haul away the rubbish.

Vacation week was a good opportunity to try to train Ozro. One day Ozro caught a tossed Frisbee. Mark praised him and kept tossing. Ozro improved each day. He caught the Frisbee at least one time out of ten. He retrieved half the tosses, and he seldom ran off to chew the disk. Ozro looked great when his big body curved in a midair leap for a catch. He was making real progress until the Frisbee disappeared from the yard where Mark had left it the night before. Nobody but the Skinners would take a tooth-marked Frisbee.

Mark was the only one home to answer the phone on Friday. In a very pleasant voice a woman asked to speak to Mr. Mark Frye. He explained that the mister of the household, Wheeler Frye, was out on the road. Mark Frye was just a kid.

"Oh, great," the voice gushed. "Then this is a real youth story. I'm Sarah Sandstone from the *Hardin Grove Herald*. I do features, and I check everything for leads, including the classifieds. I noticed a benefit sale for a youth program. Our business office referred me to you. It sounds interesting. Could I come talk to you about it? We're always looking for something positive we can report about our youth."

He held the receiver away from his ear, hoping the voice would go away.

"Are you there, Mark?"

"Yes," he whispered.

"Since you're out of school this week, why don't I come now?"

"Later would be better," Mark heard himself saying. "We've got some things to work out."

"Such as?"

"Well our budget and dog training, physical fitness and by-laws, and all."

"So you think I'd get a better story if I got in touch with you in a day or so?"

Mark assured her it would be lots better and hung up. He was relieved that no one in his family knew about the call. If he'd told Sarah Sandstone there was no program, she'd write an article about Mark Frye, biggest youth fraud in Hardin Township. But more likely she'd forget about him and write about something else.

The bill for the ad came from the *Herald* on Friday,

too. Mark slipped it out of the mail and took it and the cashbox upstairs to his desk. He set aside in neat stacks the money for the ad and for repurchase of Mom's desk and Kelli's old animals. That left one dollar and eighty cents for Mrs. McSwiggen. He recounted, added, and subtracted for half an hour. The amount didn't increase. One-eighty would be a down payment for Mrs. McSwiggen's odd lots. There was nothing left for the weights.

He was checking his figures one last time when Scott came home and called up to him to come lift weights. Working out with his big brother was great. Even on vacation Scott didn't have as much time to loaf in his tree. One thing was sure, Mark wasn't going to roll those weights back to Mrs. McSwiggen's.

Scott added five kilograms more to the bar that session, and his clean and press lift had real snap. When Mark's strenuous turn was over, he went wearily to Mrs. McSwiggen's.

He knocked hard and rattled the doorknob. He knew she was home. He could hear her radio and thuds of something being moved. Finally she opened the door. Mrs. McSwiggen was wearing baggy blue jeans and had a scarf on her head instead of her wig. There was a streak of dirt across her forehead.

"I'm glad it's you, Mark. I'm such a sight. I was ashamed to open the door." She pointed to boxes by the girls' cloakroom. "I've got more boxes ready to go. Carnival glass, Depression glass. Stock I intended for Schoolhouse Antiques. It's really too good for a flea market, but that's where it goes tomorrow."

"How was it there last week?" Mark asked.

Mrs. McSwiggen stroked her forehead with her grimy hand and left another streak. "Tiresome, but with my reasonable prices, I took in a little. Sold that dry sink. I'll bet you did well, Mark. I saw a lot of cars early when I passed your place."

"It's not finished yet exactly," Mark said. "It's just gross so far."

"Gross!" she exclaimed.

"Not that kind of gross. We still have some expenses."

Mrs. McSwiggen was tickled pink that Mark had sold most of her odd lots and books. "Every little bit helps, Mark. I figured I'll soon have regular customers at the flea market. All kinds of folks show up looking for the darndest things."

"Around those sales and auctions, Mrs. McSwiggen, did you ever see this big guy? So big he has trouble keeping his pants hitched up? Has a black truck with a blue fender."

She shook her head. "Not among the spotters and pickers I know. I'm a good picker and a fair spotter myself. Now my talents will rust. What about him?"

Mark didn't want to admit that he had made Mom heartsick and had also let a small fortune slip away. From his pocket he took coins and smoothed out a dollar bill.

"This is a down payment on your odd lots and books. I'll have to figure out how to get the rest."

Mark could tell she was disappointed at the modest sum he handed her. "I know someone who wants the weights," he said. "Could he take them now and pay later?"

Mrs. McSwiggen shook her head. "I'm not in a position to extend credit. I need cash for the weights. I guess I'll take them to the flea market. You never know who'll show up there or what they'll buy. It will be some job to get them through the crowd and into the fire hall."

Mark imagined Dirty Belly in the flea market crowd. "I've got a better idea. Leave the weights over at our house. Hire me to help you at the flea market. Instead of pay, you can give me the weights."

"You want to work for the weights, is that it?"

Mark nodded. "Yes, and the rest of your odd lots and books, too. I'll help you pack your wagon, set up your table, and I'll stay all day long or until everything is sold."

Mrs. McSwiggen dusted old picture frames. "You'd be a lot of help. Keep me from being tied to my table all day. Remember, you'd have to give up your Saturdays. Get up early. Lift and lug. Deal with the public. That takes patience. There's all kinds, Mark, I'll tell you."

Dirty Belly was sure to come. Mark would be right there to tell him the desk was sold by mistake. He'd refund Dirty Belly's money and get Mom's desk back. What's more, somebody might be selling stuffed toys like Kelli's old ones.

"Maybe you could try it for a few hours and see how you like it," Mrs. McSwiggen said.

"I'll like it." Mark was positive.

"One garage sale and you're bitten by the trading bug. All right, Mark. You can give it a try. If you get the heebie-jeebies hanging around all day, we'll work out something else."

From the schoolhouse window Mark saw Kelli come home. He was anxious to let her know he had a plan to replace her old toys. "I want to run over home and tell Kelli something," he said.

"Well, hurry back. We'll pack the wagon today and be all set for an early start in the morning."

CHAPTER ELEVEN

Mark burst into the kitchen, ready to tell Kelli about his new job. She had taken off her white apron from work and was soaking it in a basin of water. Mark felt a sudden wave of nervous anxiety that he didn't understand. Then he noticed the bottle of laundry bleach on the counter. His nose registered the smell of chlorine, which reminded him of swimming class. He'd skipped it again that week, but probably there was no class during spring break. On the other hand, the Minnows might use the extra time to swim even farther ahead of him.

Mark stood back from the counter. "Kelli, I'm working for Mrs. McSwiggen, starting now to load up for tomorrow's flea market. At that sale I'll probably see some of your old favorites and get them back for you."

"Never mind." Kelli's stopped-up nose muffled her voice. "You just get yourself out there and fill up those holes in the yard."

"Can't now. I've got a job." He hurried out to get away from the chlorine smell and back to the schoolhouse.

Mrs. McSwiggen had already started to pack the station wagon. As they worked, Mark thought of all the changes that had come since his neighbor was a little girl walking miles to a country school.

"When things got invented—the radio, TV, and all—did you understand just how it all worked?" he asked.

"Oh, great guns, no. It was all we could do to keep things running. Shorty and I usually didn't know why they ran."

"If you had to explain how some invention worked to some tribe, maybe, could you do it?"

"You betcha." She took a carton from Mark and wedged it into a tight space in her wagon. "Never throw away the instruction manual, Mark. I'd tell them to read the instructions, and if there was still trouble, call repair service." Mrs. McSwiggen rubbed the small of her back. "Sometimes it's hard just to keep yourself running. You have to feel that you have some purpose in life. That's not easy, and nobody's going to tell you what it is. You have to figure it out for yourself and hold on to it."

As Mark carried and loaded boxes, he thought about boys of the Zanzutu tribe who found their purpose when they were about Scott's age. A Zanzutu youth was sent out alone without food or water to sit on a mountaintop. At the end of three days he fell into a trance and had a dream that told him how to be a man. Going without food and water sure made a Zanzutu boy grow up in a hurry, Mark thought.

Mrs. McSwiggen brought Mark back to Hardin Road. "Remember, we're pulling out of here early before the crow flies."

On Saturday morning Mrs. McSwiggen, who didn't drive old, maneuvered quickly to beat a truck to the last good parking spot near the fire hall entrance. Customized vans, dilapidated pickups, recreational vehicles, and hatchback models jammed the parking lot.

Mrs. McSwiggen opened the back of her wagon. "Get a payday move on, Mark. The first hour of the flea market is the best."

A lot of people with their arms full tried to get into the fire hall at the same time. Mark was pushed aside first by two men carrying an oak icebox and then by a woman with a washboiler full of canning jars.

"Get behind me," Mrs. McSwiggen panted, "and hold on to that box. My old Avon bottles are packed in there."

Mark had a salt and pepper shaker collection and ten telephone-line insulators arranged on their table when Mrs. McSwiggen came with the last carton. But then she took everything off and spread the table with an old patchwork quilt, which she said was eye-catching.

Mark looked at the fire hall clock. "What's the big rush? The sale doesn't start for fifty minutes."

"Not to the public, Mark. But now's the time we buy and sell to each other. So everything ought to be out." She took a pink glass plate from newspaper wrapping. "I'm like an old war-horse. Ready to go find bargains at the other tables. But today I'm selling. I won't buy as much as a toothpick holder or a hatpin."

All the other dealers knew Edna McSwiggen, and a few bought things at her table. One woman said she had something at her booth that she knew would appeal to Edna. The price was rock-bottom.

After a while Mrs. McSwiggen began to fidget. "I'll have a look just to satisfy my curiosity. You can stay here. It would be good experience for you before the public rushes in."

Between sales he scanned the hall for Dirty Belly. Maybe he was a dealer or could just push his way in early. Mark was dismayed to see Mrs. McSwiggen returning with a grocery bag full of things. She had so much to sell, and she had bought more. She tried to appear unconcerned, but her mouth twitched as she suppressed a smile. Whatever pleased her must be at the bottom of the bag. A cloth doll in a threadbare dress was flung across the top. Its painted face was worn and cracked. It sure wasn't much. Mrs. McSwiggen hurried to put the bag under their table.

At nine o'clock Mark braced himself to deal with the public and to keep watch for Dirty Belly. Mrs. McSwiggen was cheerful as a chicadee and chatted with everyone who paused at their display. Mark wondered how she could be so pleasant to someone who handled her wares, talked about his grandmother's possessions, and then moved along without buying anything.

"They look, but they don't buy much," Mark complained.

"It's amusement, but they hope to find something. Don't look sour, Mark." She pointed to a round yellow pin among the ten-cent items. "Try to look like this happy-face button. Honey catches more flies than vinegar. We can't sell them anything if they don't stop at our table."

Mrs. McSwiggen's pricing policy was confusing. Everything was marked, but if someone asked her for her best price or if she could do a little better, she cut the price drastically. She did so for a young man with long hair who seemed very interested in an oil painting of cows in a creek. Mark held it up so the customer could see it well from a distance. He smiled until his face hurt. Surprisingly Mrs. McSwiggen didn't seem to mind when the man moved on to the next stand.

"You win some; you lose some," she said. "In this business, you have to know your values." She glanced around to make sure no one was approaching. Mrs.

McSwiggen raised the quilt that hung over the table edge and carefully drew out the old doll. One arm was gone. A leg dangled. Paint was worn off the nose.

She cupped her hand over her mouth so she wouldn't be overheard. "This is an Izannah Walker doll. Tag Mickelson has a booth on the far wall. He sold this to me for junk."

"That figures," Mark said.

Mrs. McSwiggen gently touched the doll's head. "Look at the character in that little face. Honest as the day is long. Not stuck-up or too pretty. Just character. Neat, short hair. She's in good condition, considering she's well over a hundred years old. There's not many Izannah Walker dolls around, I'll tell you. Everybody is after them. That's the latest."

"Izannah sure is a funny name," Mark said.

"Unusual," Mrs. McSwiggen corrected. "And Izannah Walker, who patented this doll, was unusual, too. Up there in her Rhode Island kitchen she figured out how to mold and harden cloth for dolls' heads. She painted these big honest eyes, nose, mouth, hair. Izannah hired a bunch of women to help her. They made over a thousand dolls that sold like hotcakes. Most of them were loved to pieces and thrown away long ago."

"Over a hundred years ago. Then how come you know all about this doll?"

"Research," she stated. "I know my values. Only a few Izannah Walkers turn up, and they are valuable."

"Like how valuable?"

Mrs. McSwiggen nudged Mark. "Four figures."

Mark was amazed. Three figures was a hundred. Four had to be a thousand dollars or more. He tried to memorize the doll's round face. He didn't ever want to miss a similar value.

"What else is in that bag? Any stuffed animals?" he asked.

"No, just some old lace curtains." She put the doll back on top of the bag and tucked it under the table cover. "We'd better not attract too much attention to that doll."

"Aren't you going to sell it?"

"Later. Not at a flea market right in front of Tag."

"Where did Mr. Mickelson get it?" Mark asked.

"You won't believe this, but he told me he found it stuffed in an old chair he reupholstered. Somebody had used it and those old curtains to replace lost stuffing. Tag knows furniture values, but he doesn't know dolls."

Mark thought of the doll's face—honest as the day is long. "But you knew. Shouldn't you have told him?"

She squirmed in her chair. "Buyer beware; seller beware. I'll tell him if my conscience gets to bothering me." She took a deep breath. "Smells like the volunteer fire auxiliary ladies are cooking up something good today. It's been a long time since breakfast."

Mrs. McSwiggen promised to bring Mark a hamburger

with everything and a piece of lemon pie when she finished her lunch at the food stand.

Since Mark wasn't busy with customers, his mind began to wander from the jumble of things offered at the flea market. He imagined the markets of the Zanzutus and decided they had one every week, and all kinds of things were traded. Fat guinea pigs were popular. He supposed, however, that the outstanding specialties of their market were the beautiful bird-feather capes. Mark thought of a neighboring tribe that had once come a long way to trade their spear-point poison for Zanzutu feather capes. That tribe would be gone now; without poison, spears wouldn't bring down much food.

He was wondering how to make spear-point poison when he smelled cigar smoke. Mark put on a big smile as a customer came near. "Hello, Mr. Bookout, looking for something special? Old maps or anything?"

Mr. Bookout regarded Mark through a haze of smoke. "Hello, Sonny. Oh, yes, I recall you came to my office with Edna. This must be her place of business. She's lucky to have a young chap like you to help." He picked up an orange glass bowl. "This is a nice carnival glass dish. I've got two hundred seventeen pieces of carnival glass."

"That kind is rare," Mark said. He was afraid Mr. Bookout would drop the bowl as he ran his shaky hands over its ruffled rim and its bumpy sides with the raised grapes design.

"You wouldn't know the name of this pattern, would you?"

"Grapes Galore." Mark was surprised at how quickly he had made up the name.

"That's a new one on me." Mr. Bookout put the bowl down and used a butter pat dish for an ashtray. "It's a downright shame Edna has to sell out this way. It surprises me she got herself in such a fix. I've known Edna since she was knee-high to a duck. Went to school with her. She was the smartest one in our class."

"Was she AT?" Mark asked.

"I don't know about that. I never heard of it, but I do remember that she was valedictorian. Got up in front of the whole town and made a speech at graduation. Then she married Shorty McSwiggen." He picked up the bowl again. "I guess I ought to buy something to help her out." He looked shocked when he turned the bowl over and saw the price mark on the bottom.

"We give a senior citizen discount," Mark asserted. "Mrs. McSwiggen's having lunch. I'll run over there and find out our best price on that bowl."

Mark knew she'd be proud of him if he made the best sale of the day. He looked for her at the crowded lunch tables. She wasn't in the food line. The woman taking orders didn't know where she was. Mark hoped she wasn't buying more things again. He gazed around the hall. No Edna McSwiggen. He'd lost the sale, for Max Bookout had moved on.

Mark's heart jumped and beat a pulse in his ears. Dirty Belly, bigger than ever, was passing their table. Mark dodged around displays of cut glass and stacks of china plates to cut in front of him.

Walking backward to face Dirty Belly, Mark spoke breathlessly. "I have to buy that pink desk back. You remember. Last week on Hardin Road. It was sold by mistake."

Dirty Belly was about to bowl Mark down as he kept on toward the exit door. "Last week is long gone. So is that old desk. I deal out of my truck. No overhead. I don't keep anything long."

"Where is it now?" Mark implored.

Dirty Belly pulled down his dirt-slicked ski jacket. "Can't say for certain. I might have sold it to a picker from the Sunbelt."

He pushed Mark aside. Before Mark could follow, somebody carrying an iron bedstead blocked the exit. He wiggled around the barrier and got to the parking lot in time to see the panel truck pulling away. Dirty Belly slowed down, leaned out of the window, and leered at Mark. "If you blister your backside, all you can do is sit on it," he shouted, and then roared away before Mark could read the mud-spattered license plate.

He remembered he was in charge of their table and rushed back inside. Mark was glad to see that Mrs. McSwiggen had returned and was still in a good mood.

"I was looking for you to get your best price on something I almost sold," he explained.

"I guess I was gone quite a spell. Got to visiting. Then there was a long line for the ladies' room. You haven't seen anything of this flea market, Mark. Eat your lunch; then have a look around."

Mark looked, but he didn't see hide nor hair of a stuffed animal until he bumped into a little girl clutching a bear that looked just like one of Kelli's. Mark asked to buy it, but the child's mother explained that her daughter never went anywhere without her bear. When the little girl began to scream and kick at him, Mark fled in embarrassment.

Finally he had only one more booth to check for stuffed toys. It didn't look promising with its display of furniture. Mr. Mickelson sat dozing in an oak rocker. He was surrounded by dressers, washstands, and more chairs. He had a desk, too.

It was glowing dark wood. Contrasting lighter wood with a patterned grain trimmed the curved rolltop and the drawer fronts. There wasn't a speck of pink paint left in the wooden keyholes or the carved fan shapes that decorated the drawers. Mark ran his hand over the curved top. It was smooth as butter.

Mark cleared his throat, and Mr. Mickelson opened his eyes.

"I see you have my mom's desk."

CHAPTER TWELVE

Tag Mickelson took a nap every day after lunch, so it was hard for him to rouse up. He was friendly enough but none too alert as Mark told him how Dirty Belly had tricked him into selling the desk his great-great-great-grandfather had made. Mark complimented him on the refinishing job and explained why the desk had been painted pink.

Mr. Mickelson shook his head and rubbed his eyes with his big hands. He thought he might still be dreaming. He claimed the desk was a fine old walnut piece with original finish. It had never been touched with a paintbrush.

Mark was shocked. Here was somebody who knew his whole family telling him a pack of lies. If he kept on insisting it was Mom's desk, most likely he'd be told to go sit on a blistered backside.

He tried to keep the anger out of his voice. "Anyhow, how much is it now?"

Tag Mickelson tapped the little white price sticker on the side of the desk. Mark looked carefully at the three figures. His anger was crushed by defeat. "Five hundred thirty-five," he said in a stricken voice. "Why is it so much?"

"For an antique burl-trimmed walnut Eastlake cylinder-front desk in original finish, that's low. I might sell it before the day's over. I saw you helping Edna McSwiggen. How's she doing today?"

Mark shrugged and went slowly back to their table. According to Edna herself, she was doing very well. Max Bookout had come back and bought the carnival glass bowl.

"So you made a fine sale, Mark. Doesn't that make you feel good?"

"Huh-uh. Maybe nothing will. Mrs. McSwiggen, don't let your conscience bother you about that valuable old doll. Tag Mickelson pretends he doesn't know what you're talking about, but he does. He buys from crooks. So what does that make him?"

"Oh, Tag's all right. I've known him a long time. He worked at the plant with Shorty." She looked closely at Mark. "You must be tired as a tick. You don't need to stay any longer. I can pack up. It won't be as much as we brought here. Run along home."

Mark was glad to get away from the flea market and

out into the spring sunshine. As he walked on the left side of Hardin Road facing traffic, he swung his jacket over his head. Working would just about ruin his Saturdays. He thought of how simple his life had been when he was ten years old. All he'd had to do then was hang around home and dig holes in the yard. He passed the vacant house where Mr. Mickelson had lived with his wife before she died. Thawing ground had left the "For Sale" sign standing crooked on the lawn.

On Saturdays the Wilderness Area was a place of peace. Mark walked under the board on the side of the bus shelter. Employment hadn't increased his height. He poked around the edge of the swamp and watched polliwogs wiggle away. He found black frog eggs held in a jellied mass and put them in a milk shake cup that had been tossed from a car. Mark tried to see how far he could throw a stone into the swamp. His pitching arm didn't seem to be any stronger.

At the Skinners' lane Ozro came lunging after a Frisbee and made a good catch.

"Ozro, drop it!" Mark commanded. "Gimme that."

Ozro wheeled around and bolted down the lane to Jack and La Vern, who urged him on. Mark was appalled. The minute his back was turned his own dog had taken up with *them*. He could work every Saturday for the rest of his life. Ozro wouldn't care. He'd just go over to the enemy.

"That's our Frisbee," Mark shouted.

"Come and get it," Jack said tauntingly.

"Prove it." La Vern grabbed the Frisbee, and both Skinners came toward him.

Mark remembered the money he had put in his pocket that morning to buy back Mom's desk and Kelli's animals. His mouth felt dry and tasted bitter. He had to stay on his feet.

Jack stuck out his foot ready to trip him if he tried to run for home. As La Vern baited him waving the Frisbee, Ozro whined and jumped.

"What's in your cup?" Jack flipped it out of Mark's hand with the Frisbee. Jellied goo flecked with frog eggs spattered Mark's face. Gobs of it hung on his shirt buttons.

While Jack and La Vern were doubled over with laughter, Mark managed to get a firm grip on Ozro's collar. He kept himself from running and walked away with as much dignity as possible. Every step brought him closer to home, as the Skinners well knew.

"You better keep your old mangy dog tied," La Vern yelled.

"Yeah. Next time we'll call the township cops." Jack hurled the Frisbee to La Vern.

Mark jerked Ozro's collar. The Zanzutus got rid of dogs that didn't mind their masters. Dumb old Ozro wouldn't last long with the Zanzutus. Finally Mark let go of Ozro, who trotted along beside him into the Fryes' yard like a model of faithfulness and obedience.

"About time you showed up." Scott sure looked big standing in the opening of the side door. He pushed his John Deere cap to the back of his head. "Come on. Let's work out with the weights."

"I'm kind of tired," Mark protested. "It's Saturday."

"You can't miss a day if you're going to get in shape." Scott took long steps toward the garage. "Say, Mark, you must have a new girlfriend. Sounds young for a change. Sarah somebody called twice. She's going to call again."

That reporter wasn't going to forget him. He'd have to think of answers for her. He didn't want to make matters worse.

Scott had a good workout, but Mark's clean and press lift was weak and wobbly. That lift sounded like a dry-cleaning service, and Mark felt as if he had been taken to the cleaner's.

"You're not concentrating. Keep your mind on what you're doing. Concentration is half of it." Scott sounded like a sportscaster.

Mark was glad when Mom came home and he and Scott could use the rest of his workout time to help carry in the groceries. They lined bags up on the kitchen counter. Scott dug a package of cheese from one sack, and Mark fished hot dogs from another.

"I wish you wouldn't eat everything before I get it unbagged," Mom said. "I remember when I could get twice this amount of food for what I spent today." She slipped a magazine from the load. "*Family Life* used to be a quarter. It's a dollar now, but I wanted to read this main article."

Beneath the cover picture of a spring salad, the headline read: TURNING YOUR HOBBY INTO A BUSINESS.

Mom perched on the kitchen stool. "I've been on the go all day, and I'd like to stop and glance at this."

"Maybe you ought to put something in the oven first." Scott went to the stove. "Want me to turn it on?"

"All right. Three-fifty." She flipped the magazine pages. "I'm always hoping to find what I *can* do that I would *like* to do. Wheeler is gone so much. Kelli's grown. Scott, you're taller than your dad. Mark's coming along. The years go so fast. Soon I won't have any family. It's like these magazines say. A woman needs something to fill those empty years."

It seemed to Mark that Mom had him grown up in an awful hurry. That didn't seem fair just because he was the youngest. He wished she wouldn't pay so much attention to magazine articles that made rules for everybody. Wearily she got up and put on her apron. Mark knew he should give her the seventeen-fifty and admit her desk was gone. He couldn't buy it now from Tag Mickelson without facing a lifetime of debt. If he told Mom how beautifully it was refinished, she'd only feel worse. He decided to wait until a better time.

Mom studied the food pages. "I don't think much of this Kraut Cake, but Tuna Ting-a-ling sounds good. I might try it for dinner." She read on. "Moderate oven for fifty minutes. I can't hold 'em off that long. Spaghetti is faster and cheaper." She turned off the oven.

Tears came into her eyes as she chopped onions for the sauce. Mark didn't know if the tears were from the onions or from her thoughts of empty years.

There weren't any old Zanzutu ladies. Some women had time to sit and weave a few baskets, but almost everyone died by age twenty-eight. Mark wondered how he could help them live longer. The thought of Mom dead and gone filled him with grief. He put his arms around her waist as she tried to work.

"Well, my goodness, Mark." Mom stroked his face with onion-smelling hands. He wiped tears from his eyes on her apron. "Now we have to get in a better mood. We can't be like this with Dad coming home."

Mark didn't want Scott to see his tears and call him a baby, so he went outside. Grass tufts that edged the holes under the pine tree were turning green. He was looking for the shovel to fill the holes when Mrs. McSwiggen drove by. Since part of his job was to unload, Mark hurried off to help her.

There weren't nearly as many boxes to carry back in as they'd had to carry out. When they finished, Mrs. McSwiggen offered Mark a glass of low-fat milk and poured herself some buttermilk. Seeing her drink it made the glands under his ears hurt. She claimed buttermilk provided the friendly bacteria her system needed.

"All in but the shoestrings," Mrs. McSwiggen said as she settled in her chair. "I did fairly well. You win some; you lose some. About average, I'd say."

"Average!" Mark exclaimed. "You won, and Mr. Mickelson lost. A doll worth four figures."

Mrs. McSwiggen sipped her sour drink. "I don't have an Izannah Walker doll. When I went to pack up, she was gone."

"Gone! What happened to her?"

"I should have been more closemouthed when I talked to you about her. Somebody heard me or caught a glimpse of that doll and knew her value. While I was waiting on trade or visiting with a dealer, some thief reached under my quilt and made off with her."

"Stole four figures? That's awful."

"No, it's not." Mrs. McSwiggen drained her glass. "My conscience was starting to nag me. I knew I'd taken advantage of Tag, but I wasn't prepared to do anything about it. Now it's taken out of my hands."

"Maybe the mall people will change their minds about your home, Mrs. McSwiggen. Their conscience will get to bothering them, and they won't take this nice place away from you."

She shook her head. "Afraid not. They're taking too much. Conscience can't handle anything so big. It breaks down like an overloaded bridge."

The Zanzutus, too, had consciences that worked only

part-time. If it rained too much or didn't rain enough, they picked a victim and clobbered him. Their consciences didn't bother them one whit. He wished he understood the highs and lows of weather better so that he could explain it and teach them to behave differently.

"You've got a faraway look in your eye, Mark. What's on your mind?"

"I was just wondering. If you had to teach people to be good, how would you start?"

"Best start with yourself. That's where I'd have to begin. In this life you must be wise as a serpent and harmless as a dove."

"But how would you start?" Mark persisted.

"Start at home," she said. "Treat your family like company and company like family."

"That sounds neat, Mrs. McSwiggen."

"And I sound like a preacher." She looked around the cluttered room. "For a while today I had myself a little dream about making a down payment on another place of my own. That's gone with Izannah Walker. I can take only a few things with me to the high rise for the elderly. I talked to a couple of dealers today. They'll take most of my big pieces. It won't take long to clear out. Then I'm taking a trip before I have to give up my wagon. I'll soon be on the road like Charles Kuralt."

"Grand Canyon." She touched the photograph on the table beside her. "I'll take a look for you, Shorty. It will be a beautiful trip in the spring."

Mark slipped out of the boys' door, leaving Mrs. McSwiggen to tell Shorty of her travel plans. Yellow daffodils bloomed at the edge of her greening lawn. He looked back at the neat white house and tried to imagine nothing there but a slab of black asphalt.

CHAPTER THIRTEEN

A fter his long day at the flea market Mark tried to stay up until Dad came home that Saturday night. Mark protested but was really relieved when Mom ordered him to bed. The next morning he was glad to see the big rig in the driveway and to hear the rumble of Dad's voice downstairs. Usually when Dad was home, Mark woke to the gurgle of perking coffee, click of dishes, sizzle of sausage. But not today. Mom wasn't humming either. She and Dad were in serious conversation.

Mark slipped down to the bottom step to listen and to learn that the subject was not himself but Kelli.

Mom knew Kelli had been under a strain working at a job she didn't like. Besides, she had to put up with her allergy and to study every spare minute, hoping to pass a test for a high school diploma. Still, it was hard for

Mom to understand why Kelli had become so worked up over algebra that she had deliberately poked runners in a good pair of panty hose. She had also thrown the only ceramic elf Mom ever finished across the room and smashed it. It was risky just to go into Kelli's room to try to help her. Mom admitted she'd never been too good at algebra and wasn't really able to help Kelli.

Dad thought he might be helpful if he were home more. He and Kelli got along great when they fixed cars. She was a smart girl, and he was surprised she didn't realize a bird in hand was worth two in the bush.

Mark sympathized with Kelli. Having both Mom and Dad mad at her was a double dose. He took the five dollars he'd set aside to repurchase her old toys, went to her door, and knocked just as if Kelli were company.

She was seated calmly at her desk in her orderly room. Mark saw no bits of broken ceramics. He went right to the point and reported that he hadn't located her scattered toys. When he offered her cash instead, she shrugged as if she no longer cared. He could keep the money. After all, he'd supplied her with the general education diploma study guide there in front of her. The toys had served their purpose. She had other things to worry about.

He watched her open a new box of tissues. "I guess the unknown fibers didn't cause your allergy. That's one of the reasons I put them in the sale."

"You could have talked it over with me." She shook her head and blew. "Of course, I didn't talk over with anybody what I did yesterday."

"What, Kelli?"

"I quit my job."

No wonder Dad and Mom were upset. Quitting a job was serious business.

Kelli told Mark she was fed up with Charley's Chicken. She needed a high school diploma to get a nonchicken job.

In the GED manual she had read of classes to prepare for the diploma test. Kelli had called the school office and learned the test was scheduled in early May. Classes to get ready for it had met since the beginning of the year and had just finished. So she had quit her job and checked a bushel of books out of the library to study and prepare for the test alone.

Kelli had to make up for lost time, especially since she had assured Rex-Tech she'd have the high school diploma required for their machinist job by the end of May. Cramming alone was dismal even for Kelli who was Academically Talented. Algebra was the worst. Hours of work, and the problems seldom came out right. Losing her temper didn't help.

"Mark, do you have any idea what X equals if X squared minus $2X$ minus 8 equals zero?"

Mark visualized a page in his math book. "If you know the equals, you have the answer. Four times eight, plus ten, minus five, equals what? That's what I'm always trying to find."

"That's arithmetic, which is sensible. Algebra is different. They tell you the answer, and you have to figure out what they put together to get it." Kelli frowned. "Or I think that's what it is."

"Maybe you won't need algebra at Rex-Tech," Mark pointed out.

"I might not. But if it works and has some order to it, I want to know what it is. I don't have a teacher every day to explain this stuff, you know."

"I'll bet Mrs. McSwiggen could. She was the smartest one in her high school class."

"That old biddy. Oh, no!" Kelli held her stomach. "Biddy makes me think of a chicken. I'd better not call her that. She went to high school a long time ago."

"Maybe algebra hasn't changed that much," Mark suggested.

Kelli wrote an equation on a clean sheet of paper and put it in the algebra textbook. "Maybe it hasn't. It's worth checking out."

Breakfast wasn't as doleful as Mark had expected. Right afterward he saw Kelli crossing the yard toward Mrs. McSwiggen's. He called after her to go to the boys' door, the one nearest the Fryes'.

Kelli stayed until Mrs. McSwiggen left for church, and she went back again in the afternoon.

Each morning afterward Kelli set off for the school-house just as if she were going to work. Mark waited a few days before he asked if his friend was a good teacher.

"Not too bad, Mark." Kelli looked pleased. "You had a good idea there. She says I'm company. Now on grammar she's dead sure, and I'm glad to know those rules instead of guessing the rest of my life. Algebra is different. We figure it out together. So we're getting it. Algebra really works. I thought the whole system was wrong, but I was wrong in the way I tried to work it."

Kelli brushed Mark's hair down over his ears. "You must be working hard, too. I hear all that thumping and groaning from the garage. You and Scott really sweat and strain."

"He's doing great." Mark imitated Scott's voice: "Come on, Mark, let's work out with the weights."

Kelli nodded. "I've noticed he doesn't have time to keep his tree limb warm."

"How about me?" Mark asked. "I have to work out with Scott, and I have to work out the weights with Mrs. McSwiggen."

Mark didn't mention his worst job. By concealment, stealth, guile, and luck, he tried to survive the bus stop abuse. Despite his daily workouts, he wasn't sure he was in shape to take on the Skinners. His first effort to test his strength had been a flop. With all his might he had charged at Jack, who was baiting him. Jack had jumped aside. Mark had gone sprawling. With the wind knocked out of him, he couldn't get up on his feet before the bus arrived.

Mom was so busy with cake decorating class that Mark knew she wouldn't notice when he skipped swimming class again. Her cake decorated with a sow and litter of pigs had won the district contest. Now she was eligible to enter the International Cake Decorating Showcase. She was very excited to be the only one in her class to qualify for this event to be held right in Hardin Grove. Three men from Canada would compete to make it international. Mom had only a week to get ready.

Mark had put in another long Saturday at the flea market. Nothing he wanted to find, not even Dirty Belly, showed up. He wondered how much longer he'd need to work before the weights were his.

Late Thursday afternoon, just two days before Mom's big cake show, Mark sat on the front step, rubbing the soft fur around Ozro's ears. He tried to think of an idea for Mom. She still hadn't decided on her subject, but she was assembling her decorating equipment.

Mom's spike heels pounded across the porch. She rummaged in her big purse and brought out a list that she stopped to study. "One more trip to Penny's for supplies. I hope I've thought of everything I'll need to-morrow to make my masterpiece. Let's see: coupler, concentrated paste, color mix, meringue powder, drop flower tip, flash nozzles, piping gel." She went toward the car in the driveway, then rushed back to shout into the house, "Scott, be sure to do your exercises." As she went by Mark, she sniffed. "Mark, you should give that big yellow mutt a bath."

At the word *bath* Ozro tried to slink away. Mark held him. "She didn't say when. It's not warm enough yet."

Mark moved to a sunny spot at the end of the step. Mom's list of supplies sure didn't make his mouth water. But he'd test the flavor of her cake the next day, when he licked the mixing bowls.

The Zanzutus had never tasted a decent cake. They had no sugar, but they had honey. So a cake might be possible. Baking powder made all those little holes in cakes. That he knew, but he wondered how to make baking powder.

Scott came to the front door. "Come on, Mark, let's work out with the weights."

"Listen, Scott, first I want to ask you something. Suppose there were these smart people. But they don't know anything about high tech. They're really low tech. And you have to teach them all about printing, computers, TV, space travel, movies, brain waves. . . ."

"No problem," Scott said. "I'd tell them there were such things. Then, if they're so smart, they could figure out everything for themselves."

"But suppose they didn't believe you?" Mark persisted.

"Come off it, Mark, you're just stalling because I'm putting another two and a half kgs on your bar today."

"Wait, Scott, have you done your regular exercises? Remember it won't be long until Dr. Feluchi sees you again. When Dad was home, I heard Mom tell him that you'd get another F in phys ed if you don't at least suit up and sit on the bench during gym."

"Mark, stay out of my business, will you? Now come on. You start with clean and press lift. The Skinners will take you to the cleaner's if you don't get in shape." The steps shook from Scott's big feet. Mark and Ozro followed him to the garage.

They had finished a pretty good workout, but Scott continued to show off his bench press. He was flat on his back, lifting, when Mom came home.

She squirmed out of the car with a big paper bag of supplies in one arm, her heavy purse on the other. She held her shopping list as she hurried toward the house. "I've got everything I wanted except one icing color. Maybe I can mix that."

She stepped into a hole and caught her heel under a tree root as she tried to break her fall. Her full weight came down on her right wrist.

"Mom! Mom!" Mark yelled as he ran to her. "Are you hurt?"

"Don't touch me," Mom pleaded when he tried to help her up. "Leave me alone for a minute." In a daze she held up her arm. The wrist was crooked.

"Scott! Mom's hurt!" Mark shouted. "Come here."

Scott took one look at Mom's wrist. "I'll call the ambulance."

Mom's face was as white as the powdered sugar that had spilled on her blue sweater. "No, call Dr. Feluchi." Mom moaned.

Scott phoned the doctor's office, and the nurse told him to get Mom to the hospital emergency room. Dr. Feluchi would meet her there.

"Kelli's at the library. I don't think I can drive." Mom sobbed.

"I can," Scott declared. "I can drive from here to Hardin Grove General Hospital without a license."

Mom held up her good hand. "No, wait, we don't want to make matters worse. Mark, get Mrs. McSwiggen."

Mark had never covered the ground between the two homes so fast. Mom was soon in the station wagon with her head leaning on the headrest of the seat.

"You're bound to feel shock, Linda." Mrs. McSwiggen's voice was calm. "I'll dodge the potholes so you can hold that arm still. We'll have you at the hospital in two shakes of a sheep's tail."

Scott motioned Mark to move over in the backseat. "I'm coming, too. I can't wait here wondering what's happening at the hospital."

CHAPTER FOURTEEN

Mark felt desolate in the hospital waiting room, which was crowded with sad, anxious-looking folks. Mom had disappeared behind a door marked "X ray." He'd seen X rays of his own teeth, but in this big hospital it seemed to Mark that X stood for the unknown. At least Scott and Mrs. McSwiggen were close to him on the hard bench.

How could things be all right one second and all wrong the next? Mom was fine coming home from shopping. The next second she was sprawled out in the yard with a broken wrist. A lot could happen in seconds.

They waited for a long time. Mark looked through old magazines without really seeing the articles, ads, and coupons. "I know what I'm going to do as soon as I get home," Mark whispered to Scott.

"I'll help you find the shovel," Scott said.

Mark turned a page to see an ad for cake mix. Mom wouldn't be in the International Cake Decorating Showcase after all.

A nurse opened the X-ray department door for Mom. Her right arm from her knuckles to her elbow was in a white plaster cast. She was pale, and her attempt to smile was one-sided. "Four to six weeks," she said.

Mrs. McSwiggen seemed to know how to treat a person with a broken wrist. She chatted away as she drove to the drug store for the pain medicine Mom might need. In the store Mark located the little bottle of pills, which pinged as the clerk slid it across a lighted x at the checkout counter. That peep was a mind-boggling mystery to him. Little stripes on the box set it off to tell the clerk the price, perhaps how many pain pills were in the store, maybe even how many pills were left in the world, for all Mark knew. He'd never be able to teach this system to the Zanzutus.

Scott asked Mrs. McSwiggen to make another stop at the supermarket for him to get frozen dinners, but she kept going. "I have a nice casserole for you to pop in the oven. A whole section of my freezer is piled with main dishes in case of company."

"That would be nice," Mom said wearily. "Kelli can cook, anything but chicken. She won't be home, though, until the library closes. I certainly thank you, Edna."

"You're very welcome to it and more. I must empty

my freezer. Everything I put up from my garden. Be ready to clear out." Mrs. McSwiggen glanced at her place as she drove on to the Fryes'.

Mom winced when she had to move her arm to get out of the wagon. "I don't know what we'll do without a good neighbor. What would I have done today? The house down the road is still vacant. There's someone down the lane with the Skinner boys, but I don't know just who it is, do you?"

Mrs. McSwiggen clicked her tongue. "Don't ask me. Those young ones have been yanked up by the hair of the head. They've been batted around from pillar to post."

Mark felt considerable satisfaction in knowing the Skinners got what they doubtlessly deserved. He stood close to hear Mrs. McSwiggen, who went on in confidential tones to Mom. "They say their stepmother's boyfriend kept them while she looked for work. They all lived in a truck, so I've heard."

"One good neighbor—for the present." Mom sighed. "With all you have to tend to now, it's a wonder you were home."

"I was doing my homework," Mrs. McSwiggen said. "I have to every day to keep ahead of Kelli."

Mom promised to let Mrs. McSwiggen know if she needed more help. Scott went home with her to get their dinner.

Mom turned on the oven in the kitchen, then went

directly to her room to lie down. Under the sink Mark found a grocery bag. He went out and gathered up all Mom's supplies. Near the garage door he found the shovel. He loosened the bare ground to fill in the holes and raked the area under the pine tree.

Then he went to Mom's room where she looked small lying on the king-size bed. The cast on her arm glowed white in the dim light.

Mark knelt beside the bed. "It's all my fault, Mom. I'm awful sorry. I filled in the holes. It only took half an hour. Just thirty dumb minutes. Like locking the barn door after the horse is stolen. That's what Mrs. McSwiggen would say."

"Yes, I guess." Mom smoothed Mark's hair down over his ears. "Or she might say, 'Better late than never.' I told you often enough. If I told you once, I told you a hundred times, but I didn't stay to see that the work was done. That's part of my job, too. At least my bone will heal. Some things won't. Four to six weeks. All spring I'll be in this cast."

"I found a grass seed bag out there, Mom, but it's empty. I'll get more and plant that bare spot. You can watch it sprout up and grow this spring. Maybe Mrs. McSwiggen has some she won't use."

"Yes, she always kept a nice yard. She's trying to be brave about leaving."

Mark patted Mom's good left arm. "I think you're

brave. Sometimes I'm not. Does your arm still hurt?"

"Yes, but I'll just have to tough it out." Mom looked at her watch. "Two hours before I can call Wheeler. He's way out in Oklahoma."

"Want me to bring you a can of pop or anything?"

"No, but I want you to put my sweater in the laundry. And throw these shoes in the Salvation Army box. That's my last pair of four-inch heels."

"Mom, sometimes I think . . ." Mark hesitated.

"Think what?" she asked.

"Oh, nothing." He picked up the shoes and sweater and stood in the doorway.

"Still thinking, Mark?"

Mark nodded. "About inventions and high-tech stuff, in case I have to teach . . . well, somebody trying to catch up. I wouldn't know where to start. Instead of trying to figure out everything in the whole world, maybe I should see if there are any holes around and start there. Fill up those holes."

Mom closed her eyes. "I don't know, Mark. I've had a hard day. I'm not sure I follow you."

"I was just thinking about this tribe." Mark stopped. Mom was right. It had been a hard day for her and for him, too. She wouldn't want to hear about the Zanzutus now.

Mark wondered if they knew how to set bones. Imagining a leg that healed crooked from an improper set, he hobbled into the kitchen, where dinner was beginning to smell good.

At school the next day Mark tried using his left hand instead of his right. Mom would sure have a terrible time for at least a month. She'd cheer up if she had her desk back. All Mark needed was five hundred thirty-five dollars. He tried his best but couldn't imagine a windfall of three figures.

Maybe Tag Mickelson would let him work out the desk the way Mrs. McSwiggen was letting him work out the weights. He'd have to slave for years. Thoughts of endless labor and debt burdened him so that he lacked his usual Friday bounce alighting from the bus that afternoon.

He was so hungry that he wished he had eaten the pinto bean muffins served at school lunch. In the kitchen he inspected the refrigerator, which contained three dozen eggs, a can of ripe olives, an opened can of tomato paste, and little else. He shook a cracker box he took from a shelf, realized it was empty, and replaced it.

By the bread box he found Mom's note, which was hard to read. She'd used a whole sheet of paper for a left-handed scrawl reading: "Kelli and I gone to watch last cake decorating class. Then groc. shop. Scott do exerc's."

Mark continued his search and looked into the bag of

cake decorating supplies. There were two boxes of cake mix on the pantry shelf. He had an idea for surprising Mom. It wasn't as great as getting her desk back, but it was sure to please her. As soon as he and Scott finished their workout, he'd make and decorate a cake for the international show.

CHAPTER FIFTEEN

Mark studied the complicated instructions on a package of piping gel cake trim. He considered decorating a flat cardboard box, which would be easier to manage than a crumbly cake. But that would be too risky. A judge might poke below the icing. He needed a base cake. Mark was careful not to tear the directions when he opened a box of cake mix.

Soon the fragrance of the baking cake made him weak with hunger. To keep himself occupied, he mixed powdered sugar, milk, and food coloring in cereal bowls. The mix of red and blue made a purple he particularly admired. The cake came out of the pan with only one tear, which he repaired on the cooling rack. It lay there looking kind of naked.

Scott came sniffing into the kitchen. "Why don't we see if that cake is as good as it smells?"

Mark could almost taste it, but he stuck to his plan. "Not now. I have to decorate it special for Mom. Not just your ordinary rose buds either."

He filled the little cloth pastry bag with purple frosting and gave it a hard squeeze. A purple mass flowed across the warm cake. According to directions, the frosting should have lain in a neat, fluted line.

"You've got it too thin," Scott said. "I'll dump more sugar in to make it thicker."

Mark sang the first lines of "America the Beautiful." "No, I like these 'Purple mountain majesties.' It's an America the Beautiful cake." Mark waved the pastry tube and sang, " 'Above the fruited plain!' Need another mountain here. Then some yellow for the fruited plain." He rinsed the purple icing from the bag and filled it with yellow, which he squeezed over the bottom of the cake. "What kind of fruit do you think it should be, Scott? Apples?" He added daubs of red icing with a spoon.

"You're really messing it up. Let me try it." Scott grabbed for the bag and trimmed his shirt cuff with yellow frosting.

Mark held on to the pastry bag. " 'Thine alabaster cities gleam,' " he sang. "What color is alabaster? Do we have any?"

"You don't have the hang of it, Mark. Leave room at

the top. I'll show you how to make spacious skies."

"Let me finish alabaster cities. Then you can do spacious skies."

By the time Scott took the bag, the frosting was beginning to harden and stick in the pastry nozzle. He intended to add a few drops of milk to the bag, but Mark bumped his arm. Scott poured in too much. The sky came out in a gush, misted the mountains, and streaked down the alabaster city.

" 'Undimmed by human tears.' But now it looks dimmed by tears." Mark stood back to admire the effect. "Still kind of pretty."

Scott tossed the empty sugar boxes in the trash. "We can't do it over. No more sugar. Anyhow, it'll taste good. Great idea making a cake for Mom, Mark. I didn't think we'd have any dessert but Jell-O for a month."

Mark wanted the cake to be a complete surprise to Mom, so he washed the bowls and baking pan. Scott didn't help him and didn't notice either when Mark went out the side door with the cake in a big pizza box. Ozro bounded around him and almost tripped him as he went to Mrs. McSwiggen's.

He had to speak up to be heard over her radio. "Could you take me to the YW? I want to put a cake in the show."

"Hardin Grove news is on now, Mark." She looked at her clock. "But the Y will close in a bit. I guess I could listen to the rest of the news on my car radio." She took her jacket from a peg in the boys' cloakroom. "There was something on the news about those big cake doings. It's nice they have a class for you youngsters."

Mark made no comment, and neither did Mrs. McSwiggen as she drove and listened to the radio. She parked at the YW and stayed in the station wagon to hear the weather report while Mark raced to the registration desk in time to enter America the Beautiful for Linda Frye.

It was the least he could do just then for Mom. Although he was anxious to get home for dinner, he would now start the harder job of obtaining her desk.

"Thanks. I just made it," he said as he got in the car. "Could we go home by way of Mr. Mickelson's? It would be a favor to Mom, sort of."

"It's considerably out of the way." Mrs. McSwiggen sounded annoyed. "But as long as I'm out and if it helps Linda."

As they drove along Westline Road, her mood changed. "I'll see if I can talk Tag into buying my freezer."

Mr. Mickelson's mobile home looked anchored. He had built on a large addition for his workshop. Its wide doors were open to give him good light to work. He seemed to be glad to be interrupted by visitors.

Mark glanced around the shop. Mrs. McSwiggen and Mr. Mickelson had so much to talk about that it was hard for Mark to get a word in edgewise. "Where's that Eastlake desk?"

"Sold it last week to a fellow who came up from Texas. He took a lot of my good pieces." Mr. Mickelson turned back to Mrs. McSwiggen as if he hadn't made the sickening announcement.

Mark wished he hadn't asked to come. Mrs. McSwiggen would gab until midnight. Aimlessly he inspected dark, scratched furniture. It was all a stack of miserable sticks looking as hopeless as he felt.

Something pink in a far corner caught his eye, and he moved two heavy chairs to get to it. Mark could hardly believe his eyes. Unmistakingly there was Mom's desk. He rubbed his finger over the scrape Dirty Belly had made on the front. A smell of dog food came from a drawer with a pellet of Chuck Wagon in one corner.

"Mr. Mickelson!" he called. "How can there be two of these just alike, except for the paint?"

Mr. Mickelson came to see what Mark was talking about. "Oh, those old desks show up every now and then around here. A lady came with that the other day. Right away she wants it refinished. It's not such a find as she thinks. She's new in Hardin Grove."

"More than one?" Mark was puzzled. "I don't get it."

"Not unlikely when you consider they were made right here in Hardin Grove at the old Forum Furniture factory," Mr. Mickelson explained. "Forum employed a lot of people here for a long time before the company moved to the Sunbelt."

Mark shut the top of the desk. "I need this for my mom. It was hers. She fell and broke her wrist. Maybe that lady could find another one that didn't need refinishing and let me buy this back for what she paid."

"I could ask her next time she bothers me to do her work ahead of everybody else. It's not promising." Mr. Mickelson shook his head. "She called this piece her pride and joy. She's furnishing their home with local antiques. They're connected somehow with the new mall."

Mrs. McSwiggen flinched at mention of the mall. All at once she looked weary enough to drop into one of the old chairs. She was through visiting and ready to go home.

On the way Mark wondered if Mom would feel better or worse if she knew that her desk had been made in a factory instead of by her great-great-grandfather.

They had Mrs. McSwiggen's Hamburger Hurrah casserole for dinner. Scott had two big helpings and then sat back as if he expected dessert. "Okay, Mark, time to serve your creation. Mom, you're in for a treat."

Mark motioned Scott into the hall. "Don't spoil the surprise. I made it for the show. It's a cake-filled world over there."

"Where?"

"The YW. I just had time to enter America the Beautiful for Mom."

Scott flung down his cap. "That mess! Nobody told you to put it in the show."

"Nobody told me not to," Mark pointed out.

"I'm telling you something right now. Mom has enough trouble without being ashamed of a cake at the show with her name on it. First thing in the morning go down to the YW and take it out."

"No can do," Mark said. "Tomorrow I'm supposed to work for Mrs. McSwiggen at the flea market. We start early."

"You get that cake out," Scott ordered.

Scott wasn't his boss. Mark was ready to tell him so, but he thought about their weight lifting. Scott might get sore at him and quit. They both needed the workouts. Scott's monthly checkup was coming soon. Mark didn't want to struggle alone with the weights. He went back to the kitchen, where Mom poured milk into a saucepan with her left hand. Mark volunteered to cook the chocolate pudding.

"What's the treat, Mark?" she asked.

He stirred and waited for the muddy liquid to thicken. "Nothing right away, but maybe sometime you'll have one of those desks. I found out that your great-great-grandfather didn't make it. It was made in a factory."

"Of course, it was made in a factory," Mom said. "The

old Forum Furniture factory that was by the millrace down on Hardin Creek. That's where my great-great-grandfather, Axel Bloomensed, got a job when he came from Denmark and couldn't speak English. He made that very kind of furniture in that factory. They paid him two dollars and fifteen cents a day. He was so happy to be earning so much that he could hardly wait until daylight so that he could go to work. That's one of the stories they told in the Bloomensed family. I guess that's why I set my heart on having that desk."

Mark held the cooking spoon over the pan. "You mean he came home from work one day with that heavy desk on his back?"

"Oh, no. I think my folks bought it at a sale around here when an old home was cleared out. I was a long time learning to appreciate it. And now it's gone."

Mom sniffed. "Mark, you're burning the pudding." She dashed to the stove and turned off the burner. Carefully with her left hand she tipped the pan to see the bottom. "Pour it out, but don't scrape the bottom."

When all the pudding with the slightly scorched flavor was gone, Mom assigned Scott the dishes and excused Mark. She said he looked worn-out and should go to bed early. Although that seemed a waste of a good April evening, Mark agreed since he had to be up early to walk to the YW before the cake show opened.

He went upstairs and fell asleep right away. With a start he woke and thought it was morning. But sounds from downstairs told him the rest of the family was still up. He'd gone to bed too early. Now he couldn't go back to sleep.

Mark thought of the story of Axel Bloomensed's first job in America. Now, and forever more, the family would add a chapter about Linda's boy Mark, who didn't ask anybody about selling, for practically nothing, one of the very desks he'd made.

Tag Mickelson would tell the newcomer about a disappointed, injured mother and a cheated child. She wouldn't care one whit. She'd insist that he get on with refinishing her pride and joy. Mark climbed out of bed and looked outside. The lights from Mrs. McSwiggen's windows were comforting. It didn't seem possible that they wouldn't always shine there.

CHAPTER SIXTEEN

In the dead of night the wind rattling the television cable attached to the house woke Mark. Drowsily he listened to rain lashing the windows. The next thing he knew, the sun was shining in his eyes.

He dressed without waking Scott and made his own breakfast. He was thankful the new YWCA was at the edge of town. Mark jumped over puddles from the night rain and jogged until he had a stitch in his side. There were only two cars in the YW parking lot.

At the entrance of the exhibition area a woman sat at a table, sorting papers. A red ribbon was stretched across the open door of the big room, where Mark saw cakes as castles, doghouses, football fields, entire villages. He didn't know if it was the sight of so much frosting or nervousness over what he had to do that made him feel kind of ill.

The woman looked up from her papers. "We're not open yet."

"Oh, that's all right," Mark assured her. "I want to take one of the cakes out. It was entered by mistake."

She looked puzzled. "That seems odd. Who entered it and under what title and classification?"

"Linda Frye, but she didn't really. The title is America the Beautiful. Only it's not exactly. It turned out kind of funny."

The woman pulled cards from a file. "Would that be it then? Humorous? We have that classification."

"No, it's not that kind of funny," Mark tried to explain. "More like strange."

She studied a card. "It's officially entered. And in an international exhibit like this we can't let one individual place an entry and another withdraw it. You can see that would get us in all kinds of trouble, can't you? Maybe if you had a written request from Linda Frye to withdraw her entry."

"She can't write."

"She's illiterate?" The woman was shocked.

"I mean, she can't write very well right now. Listen, please just let me take the cake."

"I don't know how to handle your request. I suppose a show of this scope was never put together without some hitch." She looked closely at Mark. "You do seem concerned. The general chairman will be here for the ribbon cutting and will open the show. We'll see what she says."

People began to gather around the entrance, crowding Mark against the red ribbon. Just one duck, and he could be under it, find his cake, and run. Could he make a clean getaway? He imagined the sticky scramble among the cakes as he was pursued by cake show officials, Hardin Grove police, and reporters. It could be an international incident.

The entrance was packed for the opening ceremony. Then Mark found himself moving along with the crowd into the exhibit. He'd never seen such heights of frosting: a mountain complete with skiers, Mount Rushmore with sculpture. Snoopy was there on his doghouse, and Oscar the Grouch in his garbage can.

"Mark, what are you doing here?" Mark was so startled to hear Kelli's voice that he almost jabbed his fist into a Three Bears cake. Mom was with her.

"Well . . ." Mark stammered. "You're here early."

"I could hardly wait until the show opened to see what other folks entered." Mom straightened Mark's hair. "You're the early one. I didn't realize you were so interested in this. We thought you were helping Mrs. McSwiggen."

Mom was puzzled when two friends from her cake decorating class complimented her. "I don't know why they are congratulating me unless it's for breaking my wrist instead of my neck." She looked at more cakes. "These are so beautiful. See this one, a perfect formal garden." She turned over the entry card with an honorable mention ribbon attached. "I learn a lot from reading the judges' comments on these cards."

Out of the corner of his eye Mark saw a purple blur. America the Beautiful was on the next table. The judges had probably written mean things on the card. "Aren't you getting tired, Mom? Arm hurt? Maybe we'd better go," Mark suggested.

"Oh, no, I'm enjoying it." Mom read another card.

He took her left hand. "Come over here and tell me how a whole circus was made of frosting."

"Don't rush me. First I want to see the entries here on this next table." She moved on. "I don't always agree with the judges. This one, for instance."

Mark's heart sank as she flipped over the entry card of America the Beautiful. Then he was amazed to notice a blue ribbon dangling from the card. Along with Mom he read the penciled comments: "Very original. Bold use of color. Creative design carries feeling of freedom and is refreshing departure from the oversentimental. Clever title."

"Hmm. I don't know about all that. Whose entry is this?" Mom turned the card over and read her own name.

Another woman congratulated Mom as she stood holding the card, looking as sickly sweet as if she'd eaten half a cake.

"I wanted you to have a cake to show," Mark said. "Scott and I were just fooling around, but look, you won first prize for creativity. Congratulations."

"But I didn't do it." Mom's voice was tense and low. "I can't accept the award. This whole class will have to be rejudged. I'll have a lot of explaining to do."

"That will be hard," Mark said. "They don't know how to handle anything unusual here."

Kelli squinted her eyes. "It's like a modern painting. If you make a fuss, Mom, you'll make the judges look silly. Why don't you just let it stand? It sure looks as if you did it with your left hand."

"Don't give me away." Mom covered her mouth with her hand. "If it leaks out that this isn't my work, our whole international show will be disqualified, and all awards revoked."

"Nobody wants a hullabaloo like that," Kelli said. Mom agreed as they moved on to the next table.

Mom put her good arm around Mark's shoulders. "Congratulations, Mark. You got an award on the first cake you ever decorated. You should get a second one for thinking of your mom and doing something for me. I know you didn't realize this contest has a pack of rules."

They were supposed to be quiet on the way home so Kelli could diagnose a motor knock in the car as she drove. Mark leaned over the front seat to whisper to Mom, "Any prize with the blue ribbon?"

"Sure. *You* won twenty dollars' worth of cake decorating supplies."

He wasn't thrilled, but a prize was a prize. Mark had never before won anything. Mom seemed content, and Scott couldn't complain about the outcome of entering.

They crossed the bridge over Hardin Creek, which was swift and muddy from the night rain. By contrast the day was tranquil and bright. Mark wished he wasn't scheduled to spend the best part of it at an indoor flea market.

He was happy to see Mrs. McSwiggen at her mailbox. She must be skipping the flea market. At Mark's request Kelli stopped. "Since she's home, Mark, ask her when I can come to check my math sheets."

Mrs. McSwiggen assured Mark that she would be around all day. She still had some big pieces of furniture, but she'd sold most of her small items and wanted a Saturday away from the flea market.

At the edge of her garden she picked up a handful of loose soil. "What I'd really like to do this morning is put in a lettuce bed. Plant radish seeds and onion sets."

"I hope you can stay and raise more veggies than you can eat. Has your lawyer found you a loophole?"

"Doesn't look too good." She straightened her shoulders. "But I'm not going to whine over it and complain the rest of my life, however long that may be. I'm getting everything in order. That's what you have to do. Know you might die tomorrow and keep going as if you would live forever. It's tricky, I'll tell you."

Mark remembered a program on television, *Nova* maybe, that he'd seen about time and space. If humans could travel in space at the speed of light, they would somehow get out beyond time and never grow old. He pictured Mrs. McSwiggen in her weekend wig and peach-colored pants suit speeding through space forever. He wasn't sure she'd like it.

Certainly the Zanzutus wouldn't believe this theory. If he tried to explain it, they would think evil spirits had possessed him. They had crude ways of dealing with evil spirits. He'd best skip talk of outdistancing time.

When Kelli came over with books and papers, Mark wandered off beyond the parts car to the far edge of the Frye place. Their last Christmas tree lodged against the back fence still held a few brown needles.

Mark thought of the vacant land between his home and Hardin Creek as the Outback. The idea had come to him during study of Australia at school. His Outback had once been cultivated fields. Now weeds and brush were moving in.

He and Ozro hadn't traveled into the Outback since last fall. The dog run gate was open. Mark called and called. His voice echoed back to him, but his dog didn't appear.

Mark hopped over the rusty fence and felt like a

Zanzutu boy as he followed a trace of path. It would be as good as I-90 to the Zanzutus, who had no cars, trucks, not even horses. They wouldn't need much of a road for a while at least. Eventually he'd explain expressways to them. He wasn't sure of the recipe for concrete, but he could show them how to make a clover-leaf entrance and exit.

He considered Scott's idea of letting the Zanzutus figure things out for themselves. He'd give assignments: Barlanoo, you're on telephone circuits; Ketchiku and Cuti, jet engines; Inyu, antibiotics. All assignments due in a month.

He stumbled over a stone that bordered sunken ground. The stones were all that remained of a house foundation. Some had fallen into the cellar hole. Mark could not remember the house, which had tumbled down long ago. The nearby lilac bush leafed out fresh and green every spring. He stopped to examine the tender heart-shaped leaves and the dark clusters of flower buds.

A spot of bright orange caught his eye. He picked up a Frisbee pocked with tooth marks and put it under his arm. The Skinners had doubtless used it to lure Ozro away.

He thought of the big sycamore tree that grew near the bridge and wondered if it was greening out with fuzzy leaves. He supposed sycamores bloomed in the spring. From articles he'd read in a nature magazine he knew that something had to produce those little balls that trimmed sycamore trees in the fall.

The big tree with its white limbs against the blue sky was easy to locate, but Mark couldn't get near it. Hardin Creek had overflowed its banks and flooded all the low ground around the tree. The island near the creek's shore had shrunken to a patch of ground above water. He watched driftwood wash down and lodge against the sycamore tree.

Above the water's roar he heard yells and barks. Three heads showed above a curved black shape, glistening like a shark, that bobbed downstream. Two of those heads had to be the Skinners. The third one was Ozro.

The big truck inner tube was swept into the current, where it tipped and rocked. A sheet of blue plastic came loose from the tube and churned off behind it. The yells of excitement turned to screams of alarm.

The patch of island split the current and brought the tube nearer the bank. Jack had an arm around the rim. La Vern was about to lose his grip. Ozro scrambled onto the slippery rim. Mark could hear his pitiful whine. His leap off the side upset the tube. Jack and La Vern were thrown into the cold, foaming water.

For a moment Mark couldn't tell what was happening amid the splashing in the swift water. The current swept Jack near shore, where he caught hold of overhanging willow branches. He reached out and grasped La Vern. Ozro swam hard toward the bank.

The Skinners pulled themselves along the limber willow boughs to the muddy water's edge, where they stood dripping and shivering. Glad as Mark was to see Ozro reach land, he stood away from him until he gave himself a good shake.

Jack's lips were blue. "Your old dog tried to drown us."

La Vern's teeth chattered. "Yeah. He knew we couldn't swim. He pawed our plastic liner and made it come loose. Now we'll catch it. Lost a truck tube. All his fault. We'll get you both."

Mark was furious. "You leave Ozro alone. And you leave our Frisbee alone, too."

Quick as a wet lizard, Jack slipped the Frisbee from under Mark's arm. "You want your old Frisbee; go get it." He threw it into the creek. The fight had gone out of them just then, but the Skinners still had a measure of meanness. Water ran down their backs and squished in their sneakers as they walked away.

At least Ozro didn't follow them. He paced and whined, watching the Frisbee swirl without direction in the backwater eddy.

"Stay, Ozro," Mark commanded. "You got out of there once. You're a lucky dog."

The current caught the Frisbee and carried it into the main stream. Ozro whined anxiously. Suddenly he lunged in. His towhead and shoulders were just above-water. Ozro didn't splash, but Mark could tell by the movement of his shoulders that he was swimming with all his might. The Frisbee was just ahead of him in the swift current.

"Here, Ozro, come back, Ozro!" Mark yelled. But Ozro couldn't turn now. His strength would soon give out in the choppy cold water. Ozro, his own dog, was leaving him. He'd drown in Hardin Creek. Just when Mark felt completely hopeless, the current cast Ozro onto a bit of land no bigger than the bed in his doghouse. He shook and hunkered there with the Frisbee in his mouth.

"Ozro, you dumb, stupid dog, you can just stay there. Stay until you starve to death." Tears rolled down Mark's face as he yelled. "I'll get the township cops to come after you. Sometime next week."

To Mark's dismay Ozro turned and turned as if ready to jump into the stream again. "Ozro, stay! Stay! You hear me? I'll get Scott to help."

Ozro plunged into the water and swam hard toward Mark, but the current carried him downstream. Mark jumped over brush and scrambled through brambles to get ahead of him. He crept out on a tongue of grass-covered bank and reached out as far as he dared. Just as he grasped Ozro's collar, the earth, undercut by the current, collapsed.

The cold took Mark's breath away. Muddy water choked him. He tried to stand, but his feet touched nothing. Mark clawed the raw earth bank that slipped away. With all his strength he thrashed his legs, flailed his free arm, and gasped for breath. His wet clothes dragged him under. His knee struck something firm. He could stand. Swift water knocked him down twice as he floundered to the bank, where both he and Ozro lay panting.

Too exhausted and shocked to sit up, Mark took deep breaths of wonderful air that smelled of earth. Something rattled beside his ear. Ozro was dropping and picking up the Frisbee.

"Never mind, Ozro," he said in a weary voice. "A Frisbee is not that important." Mark propped his head on his elbow. "Did I save you, or did you save me, you big, yellow, disobedient mutt?"

After a long rest Mark walked slowly home through the Outback. The sky had never been so blue. He loved every blade of grass. Like a dog on a short leash, Ozro stayed close beside him.

Mark was anxious to slip into the house and change his wet, muddy clothes without being noticed. He didn't want the Outback to be declared off-limits. He stayed home and was helpful the rest of the day. The many jobs he volunteered for included doing two loads of laundry for Mom. He was so busy that Mom wondered how he'd found time to give Ozro a bath.

When Mark stretched out his legs in bed that night, he felt a wave of fear like the panic that had gripped him when he couldn't touch bottom. He closed his eyes and saw swirling, muddy water. Mark imagined Ozro's long, lifeless body stretched out on a pile of driftwood. There would be a big double funeral when they found the bodies of Jack and La Vern. His family would have to go to visiting hours, which would be hard for them just after Mark's own sad funeral.

None of it had happened. The dusk-to-dawn light shone on the pine branches outside the window. His soft comforter covered him. He was safe at home.

Being alive was wonderful. All kinds of people everywhere should be alive. Somehow he'd stay alive during the coming week even if the Skinners were out to get him. One thing was for certain: He wouldn't skip swimming class. He'd beg the teacher for makeup instruction. He wouldn't mind if he were put back into the baby Tadpole group; he'd be there.

He closed his eyes and tried to sleep. Again he saw swift, muddy water. Across the room Scott was already breathing deeply in sleep. Mark hopped out of his bed and crawled in beside him. There wasn't much room. He put his hand on Scott's side and felt his deep, rhythmic breathing. Being able to breathe was marvelous. He wanted to wake Scott up and thank him for being there.

CHAPTER SEVENTEEN

Right after breakfast the next morning Mark rushed to Mrs. McSwiggen's. He wanted to know if she'd heard Mom's name broadcast on the local news as a cake award winner. The wide door of the woodshed was open. The station wagon was gone. He wondered where she could be so early Sunday morning.

Notices were tacked to both her doors. Mark read the printed No Trespassing signs: VIOLATORS WILL BE PROS-ECUTED TO THE FULLEST EXTENT OF THE LAW. He couldn't read the scrawled signature at the bottom, but his title, vice president of Distribution Development, Inc., was plain enough.

There were no curtains at the windows, so he could easily see inside. He was shocked at the change. Dust particles floated in shafts of light that fell on the bare floor. The stove and refrigerator were still lined up against the blackboard, but the remaining furniture was out of place. Four bulging plastic garbage bags were piled in a corner. All the pictures and knickknacks were gone. Mrs. McSwiggen had departed without telling him good-bye.

His desolate feeling changed to relief when she came driving home. "Oh, Mrs. McSwiggen," he called, "I was afraid you were gone for good."

"Not quite. I wouldn't go without bidding you farewell, Mark. Kelli, too. I'll have to tell her I won't be here to finish cramming for her GED test." Mrs. McSwiggen looked at her doors. "I hate to go in there. It looks so miserable. I've already taken two loads of things I can't live without to Tag Mickelson's for storage. He was nice to take it in, considering I was too proud to tell him how I lost my place. I feel like such a fool. The rest of the furniture is sold; it'll be picked up."

"Where are you going?"

"Grand Canyon. I'm starting this morning. I made up my mind in a hurry after he put up those signs yesterday. Peck, peck, I heard and thought at first it was a woodpecker. It was the same man who came when you were here. He didn't have the manners to tell me what he was doing. Peck, peck, just like that."

Mrs. McSwiggen was steeled to go inside when Kelli came stepping high and looking extra pretty.

Kelli opened her notebook. "I remembered what you said, Mrs. McSwiggen, 'The better the day, the better the deed.' I've done the equations and grammar exercises you assigned. I thought you might have time to check them before you go to church."

Kelli was terribly disappointed to learn that Mrs. McSwiggen was leaving and declared the No Trespassing signs downright rotten.

"When will you be back?" she asked.

Mrs. McSwiggen shook her head. "No telling."

Kelli opened her manual. "We didn't have much more to do. I don't think I can make it without you."

"I'm sorry, hon. You were going so well. Heaven knows I'd like to stay, but I haven't lived in a house with signs on the doors since we were quarantined for scarlet fever when I was eight years old."

Kelli was downcast when she thanked Mrs. McSwiggen for helping her. Mark reminded Kelli that she had been Academically Talented, but that didn't cheer her up. When she left, she was as dejected as she used to be when she faced a shift and a half at Charley's Chicken.

"I've got my food cooler packed," Mrs. McSwiggen said. "Give me a hand, Mark."

Mark struggled to hold up his end of the heavy red cooler as they carried it to the station wagon. Then he toted out a heavy suitcase. There might be more to come, so he went back inside, where Mrs. McSwiggen thrust into his hands a potted plant with mottled tall, stiff foliage. He held it carefully to prevent poking himself in the eye with its spears.

"Give that to your mother. I'm leaving her my sansevieria for a keepsake. She claims plants die for her. She can't kill that one." Mrs. McSwiggen took a sheaf of coupons out of her jacket pocket. "These are for your mother, Mark. Tell her to use them before they expire." She looked back into the forsaken room. "Expire. A lot of things are expiring. Coming to an end." She straightened her shoulders. "Just as long as I don't expire. I'm tough as that sansevieria plant. Old sansevierias sometimes bloom."

She was ready to go. Mark felt empty and helpless as he went ahead of her out the boys' door. The sound of the lock echoed in the nearly empty room as she closed the door behind her. She put her tote bag down and stood rigidly on the step with her back to her old home. She wore her wig and her navy blue travel suit. Her earrings, eyeglass frame, and neck chains sparkled in the sun. Rouge on her cheeks and red lipstick wider than her thin lips stood out on her pale face.

"I won't look back." As she picked up her tote bag and walked to the station wagon, her red mouth was a little twisted.

Mark didn't look back either. He'd go feed Ozro, work out with Scott, plant grass seed under the pine tree, help Mom, keep as busy as he could all day.

The schoolhouse seemed shrunken and forlorn without Mrs. McSwiggen coming and going. Mark tried not to look that way when he got off the school bus in the afternoons during the next week. He wanted to tear the signs off the door but decided that wouldn't really change anything. After all, Mrs. McSwiggen had left them there.

Mark didn't dare miss a day working hard with the weights. He couldn't tell what the Skinners were up to. One morning they pretended to be good buddies and whacked him on the back hard enough to jar his lungs loose. The next day they threatened to waylay him at a time and place no school bus could save him. On Wednesday they peeled off his jacket, went through the pockets, and threw it in the swamp. Another day they did nothing but whistle until the bus came. Shrieking, "Watch your step," they shoved him into the bus so that he landed on his knees by the driver. That was the big joke of the day at school.

Scott worked out with the weights willingly, but he got crankier as the time for his checkup came nearer. Mom had to ask him three times to vacuum for her so the house would be clean when Dad came home. He was due home a day early so that he, too, would hear what Dr. Feluchi would say on Saturday about Scott's back. Kelli was glum because she thought she might have to put off her GED test for another whole year. Mom with her arm in a cast was in the best mood. She was pleased when she tried to straighten Mark's damp, matted hair the day he got a ride home from swimming class.

Mark had a nervous feeling in the pit of his stomach

when he thought of facing Dad for the first time since Mom's accident. He would tell Dad right away the plot of a book he was reading and also anything else he could think of to get Dad's mind off the holes he'd left in the yard. Still, he knew that sooner or later Dad's weary, accusing look would dwell on him.

Ozro barked wildly when Dad's rig rolled in near dinnertime on Friday. Mark had decided to meet his problem head-on. As soon as Dad climbed down from the cab, Mark threw his arms as far as they'd go around his waist. "Dad, it's my fault Mom got hurt. I didn't mind any better than Ozro. I'm awful sorry."

Dad's stomach growled, and so did his voice. "Being sorry won't make a bone knit or pay for the emergency room. It'll help some if you've learned what neglect can do." He loosened Mark's arms. "Some things take care of themselves. Leave 'em be. Other things don't." He patted the truck hood. "If our living here begins to pound, steer hard, I know it won't fix itself. I have to find the trouble. Take care of it." He reached into the cab and brought out a large plant with clusters of pink blooms big as grapefruits. "Do you think Mom will like this? Hydrangea, the fellow I bought it from called it."

Mom hugged and kissed Dad and cried a little the way she did when he'd been on the road a long time. Then she talked a blue streak while looking around for a place to put the big plant.

Mark waited for a chance to tell Dad about Mrs.

McSwiggen. He tried to think of her leaving in terms he'd often heard—moved away, gave up her place, had to make a change. He thought saying such ordinary phrases might make him feel better.

Everyone except Mark was on a schedule the next morning. Kelli had an appointment with her doctor, whom she called a sneeze and wheeze specialist. Mom, Dad, and Scott knew they'd spend a lot of time in Dr. Feluchi's crowded office, first for Mom's wrist, then for the conference about Scott's back. After they all had left and the house had settled down, Mark sat on the porch step with Ozro. He noticed that grass was coming up in the bare spots as thick as the hair on Ozro's back.

To his surprise a big truck turned into Mrs. McSwiggen's drive. He and Ozro ran to the schoolhouse and watched the driver ease a huge bulldozer down the flatbed trailer ramp and roar it up to the girls' door. The driver tried the locked door, then crushed a clump of daffodils underfoot when he looked in a window.

"They've got their wires crossed. This place hasn't been cleared out yet. Do you know where the party is who owns this furniture?" he asked as if he'd just noticed Mark.

Mark shook his head. "It isn't a party. Just one lady, Edna McSwiggen."

"Whoever. I can't waste my time waiting around here. I'll be back later."

"What are you going to do?" Mark's voice quivered.

"My orders are to knock 'er down." He looked at the little gleaming white schoolhouse. "It's been standing here a hundred years or more. Ten minutes after I hit it with that 'dozer blade it'll be a pile of kindling."

All too well Mark could imagine the sorry sight. The Zanzutus didn't care much about buildings. In fact, they burned a home if someone died there so that the spirit couldn't come back to the house. So maybe a building wasn't so important. But Mrs. McSwiggen's dream would be knocked over and flattened along with her schoolhouse.

The heavy, scarred blade of the yellow bulldozer made the white clapboards look fragile. Mark didn't want to be around when the bulldozer roared again.

Aimlessly he started down Hardin Road. Ozro followed until sight of a woodchuck by its den lured him into the Outback. Mark went on and came to the turn for Westline Road. Maybe, just maybe, Mr. Mickelson's customer had agreed to return Mom's desk. He turned into Westline and knew he was in for a long hike. At least Tag Mickelson might want some company, just as Mark did.

Mom's desk looked like a skeleton in Mr. Mickelson's work area. All the drawers had been taken out and stacked aside. Mr. Mickelson was carefully using a hand scraper on the top.

"I guess I can stop for a minute." He held out his dusty hand to Mark. "That dame won't see me. She's been pestering the daylights outa me. I had to start her job. It'll be considerable work, too. That desk hasn't been properly repaired. Needs a good going-over."

"Did you ask her if she'd sell it?"

"Sure, but she says she has just the place for it." He picked up a small drawer. "This is still the original finish. It goes inside the rolltop beside the pigeonholes. When I started work, I noticed it didn't close right. I figured it needed repair. I pulled it out and found this jammed behind it." He took a folded piece of yellowed paper from his shirt pocket. "By rights it belongs to her, but she's been a pain. I think I'll give it to the Hardin Grove Historical Society."

He handed the paper to Mark. Hard-to-read, old-style handwriting in faded ink stated: "For consideration of one dollar, I hereby sell to Hardin Creek School District as site for school building with access to public road, two acres, more or less, from the northeast corner of my property situated in Hardin County, Pennsylvania. M. L. Hardin, January 9, 1848." Mark was too excited to study the sketched map with distances, angles, and landmarks shown.

"Mr. Mickelson, please, can you give me a ride home? This is important."

"Been around since eighteen forty-eight, so I guess there's no hurry." He picked up his scraper. "I've got a job to do here."

"Come on, please. This is what Mrs. McSwiggen needed," Mark insisted.

"Long before her time." Tag Mickelson kept scraping. Plainly he didn't always know values. "May I borrow this?" Mark didn't wait for an answer as he set out in a dead run.

CHAPTER EIGHTEEN

Mark sprinted until he was breathless. His mouth was dry as cotton, and his side ached. The sun beamed down. His jacket was a nuisance. Sweat running into his eyes made the roadside trees jiggle. He realized he had to slow down and pace himself if he was to finish the run.

Near Hardin Road he flung himself down on the grass at the edge of the road. Hunger and exhaustion made him feel faint. He closed his eyes and saw a pile of kindling. He'd allow himself a breather of one more minute.

An awful jolt struck his back. A grip around his neck choked him. Jack jumped out of the roadside brush. "Hold him, La Vern! He's in no hurry. No school bus coming. No big brother. Long way from home. Let's see what's in his pockets."

A jolt of anger hit Mark harder than La Vern's big hulk. The Skinners wouldn't get their hands on M. L. Hardin's paper and tear it to bits. They wouldn't delay him from saving the schoolhouse. Mark gathered all his strength, gritted his teeth, and broke free.

La Vern was dumbfounded. "What's got into him?"

Jack doubled his fists and blocked Mark's way.

"Let me by," Mark yelled. "They're going to tear down my friend's house."

"Wow! I want to see that." Jack's punch didn't connect.

Mark's did, and he kept on swinging without knowing whom he hit where. His mouth was bone dry. Mark's jaw ached from a hard jab, and his nose stung. He had to stay on his feet and keep fighting.

The Skinners retreated to the middle of the road to block his way. A helicopter chopped overhead. In the second that Jack glanced upward, Mark charged into him. La Vern was so amazed to see Jack flattened that he didn't ward off Mark's blow to his stomach.

Mark wanted to run like a rabbit but held himself to a dignified walk past the Skinners to the first turn in the road. When he heard no footsteps following, he wiped his bloody nose on his sleeve and ran faster than ever.

He rounded the big curve in Hardin Road and caught a wonderful glimpse of the bell cupola among the budding treetops. He risked slowing to a jog. The whole building was now in sight. The schoolhouse stood but was still in danger. Too many trucks, cars, and people were gathered around.

According to the name on the door, the van in the drive belonged to the *Hardin Grove Herald*. Mark recognized the black truck with the blue fender beside the bulldozer. The flatbed truck was back, parked on Mrs. McSwiggen's lawn.

The bulldozer operator lounged against his equipment, talking to Dirty Belly. A young woman whom Mark remembered seeing at the *Herald* office listened to their conversation. Her bracelets jingled as she pushed back her long hair and wrote in her notebook. A fellow was in Mrs. McSwiggen's garden, taking pictures of the schoolhouse.

"Wait! Stop!" Mark panted for breath.

They stopped talking long enough to joke about Mark's looking as if he'd been in a battle. Then the bulldozer operator moved his arm in a leveling motion. "Put in the curbing; take the trees out; pour the blacktop. Finally get this place looking good."

"I took in two sales and cleared out another place today," Dirty Belly announced. He opened the back of his truck. "Little late, but I'll get this junk out of your way now."

"No hurry. Working or not, I get fifty-two fifty an hour for this baby." The operator patted the bulldozer. "My orders are to take 'er down when all contents are out. Won't take long for this little job."

Mark bumped the young woman's notebook. "I live next door. Mark Frye. Listen, they're making a big mistake. I can prove it."

"Oh, hi, Mark. I'm Sarah Sandstone." She kept scribbling. "I've been trying to get in touch. No answer when I phoned, so we came by on the chance you'd be around somewhere. I'll talk to you later. Right now the photographer and I must cover this story I just stumbled onto. End-of-an-era kind of thing."

Dirty Belly turned the knobs of both doors. "The old woman said everybody around here was honest and the place would be open. Now she's gone and locked me out."

"Musta locked up from force of habit," the bulldozer operator said.

Dirty Belly stood back. "Ain't no problem."

Mark jumped in front of him, waving the precious document. "Wait! This was in that old desk you gypped me out of."

"Boy, you bug me. Watch out." Leading with his thick shoulder, Dirty Belly charged full force into the door. He lunged again; wood splintered. Two hard kicks, and the door opened.

Mark didn't want to see inside and turned away. A car came slowly down the road as if the driver and passenger were looking for something. No siren blew. No light circled and flashed, but Mark recognized the township police. He ran to the end of the driveway, where the car stopped.

A policeman leaned his head out the passenger window. "Have you seen a big yellow dog running loose? We've had a report on one."

"Make them stop!" Mark yelled. "It's Mrs. McSwiggen's house. M. L. Hardin gave it to her—I mean to the school district. It says so right here." Mark gave him the document.

He glanced at it and handed it to his partner in the driver's seat. "Yes, we know Edna McSwiggen. Where is she?"

"Grand Canyon," Mark answered quickly.

"Looks like she'd better stay home and tend to business." The driver passed the paper back to Mark. "And we'd better catch that dog seen in this neighborhood. Complaint said he tore up a pea patch."

"She was tending to business," Mark insisted, "but I found this, well, Mr. Mickelson found this after she left."

"Nice souvenir, but too old to mean anything in this day and age." The driver started the car. "Anyhow, it's a civil case. We don't get into that. We've got too much as it is with crime, traffic-related cases, dog-law enforcement. We'll cruise by the old fields, see if that dog is down there digging out a woodchuck."

"Traffic-related? Dirty Belly came in his truck. Breaking and entering." Mark shoved with his shoulder to demonstrate. "Wham! He broke the door down, and there was a No Trespassing sign on it."

"Who do you mean?" the driver asked.

"That big guy carrying Mrs. McSwiggen's dresser out on his back."

"As long as we're here, I'll take a look." The driver shut off the motor and turned up the police radio. "You can audit the box."

The policeman strolled up the drive. "Everything all right here?"

"Yes. Just waiting until the place is cleared out." The bulldozer operator glanced at his watch. "Then down she comes."

The policeman watched Dirty Belly heave the dresser into the truck. "Do you have a receipt for the items you're taking? Some kind of bill of sale?"

"We don't do business that way. I take everything. Doing the old woman a favor. Lotta junk. I'll haul most of it to the landfill." He scratched his big belly.

"The building is going to come down, so you might be in the clear on property damage," the policeman said, "but I'll have to see a receipt for sale of contents."

Dirty Belly took a mess of papers from his truck dashboard and thumbed through them. "See if my bookkeeping system works. Yeah. It's here. She remembered to give it to me. Then she locked me out."

The policeman read the slip of paper. "Vague, but I guess everything is paid for."

Dirty Belly's fat jowls split in a gap-toothed grin. "I wouldn't be bustin' a gut taking it out in broad daylight before witnesses if it wasn't, would I?"

The police radio squawked another report about the uncontrolled big yellow dog. "We've got a job to take care of, and everything appears to be in order here." Still, the policeman seemed in doubt and walked around the truck.

Mark looked into its dusty dimness. Over the edge of a cardboard box two eyes peered at him. They were honest as the day is long. He drew the doll out and recognized the print of her tattered dress and the pattern of cracks on her painted cloth face.

"Izannah Walker!" Mark shouted, "He's got her. She was kidnapped from Mrs. McSwiggen."

Dirty Belly tried to snatch the doll from him.

"Watch out. She's a valuable antique." Mark carefully handed Izannah to the policeman.

He studied her honest eyes. "Where did you get this?"

"Picked it up somewhere. Piece of trash."

"He picked her up at the flea market from under Mrs. McSwiggen's table," Mark accused. "Not trash either. She's worth four figures. That's grand larceny."

"Where's your sales slip for this?" the policeman asked.

"We don't do business that way." Dirty Belly tried to smile again, but his jowls were too heavy.

"You've got a broken taillight. Your vehicle inspection sticker has expired, and your tail pipe is dragging." The policeman was writing a ticket. "I'll have to cite you for that. And we've got this possession of stolen property charge. You're going with us to see the district magistrate. It won't take long."

"Too long for me." The bulldozer operator kicked a big tire. "I've got to referee a Little League game. See you next week."

Mark felt joy take hold of him and spin him around. Next week was time enough for the document to do its work.

As the policeman walked down the drive, Izannah Walker's legs dangled from under his arm. Dirty Belly's arms stuck out like a doll's arms from his barrel body. You could never tell what kind of person would know values.

Mark was exhausted but contented as he sat on the schoolhouse step. Heavy paws landed on his shoulders, and a big, wet tongue slobbered his face. He grabbed Ozro's collar and pulled him out of sight behind the bulldozer just as the policeman turned to get in his car.

With hair flying and bracelets jangling, Sarah Sandstone rushed to the van. "I won't need to interview you just now, Mark. This is a better story."

CHAPTER NINETEEN

The Hardin Township police drove off, followed by the van and the flatbed truck. Dad was so curious about the traffic and the bulldozer that he stopped the Chrysler at the schoolhouse, and Mark's whole family piled out.

Mark had just enough time to dash to Mrs. McSwiggen's sink and wash his face before Dad appeared at her splintered door, asking, "Mark, what the Sam Hill is going on?"

Mark gasped, sputtered, and almost choked on his words in his excitement. He kept his arms folded so Mom wouldn't notice the blood on his shirt. Dad promised to get in touch with Max Bookout right away about Mrs. McSwiggen's place.

Although Mom smiled and nodded, she only half listened. "I just can't get over this day. I'll never have my old desk, but I'm glad it was useful. Wheeler, I've been so worried. Isn't it great? Remarkable improvement."

Now it was Mark's turn to listen as Mom quoted Dr. Feluchi. " 'Well-developing back musculature. Exceptional progress. Remarkable improvement. No operation!' Wheeler, you heard Dr. Feluchi. We won't even need to wear a brace."

Scott stood straight and tall. "We? Where do you get that *we* stuff?" he joked. "Mom, it's way after twelve. When are we going home to dive into that fifteen-incher we got at Pizza Villa?"

Mom looked around. "We could have a picnic right here. Mrs. McSwiggen has such a nice yard, and it's a beautiful day. Get the pizza, Scott."

"What about your wrist?" Mark touched her cast.

"Doing fine. The cast will come off a week sooner than Dr. Feluci expected. Mark, keep that big yellow mutt out of the pizza while I go in and see if I can borrow a knife and whatever we need from Mrs. McSwiggen."

Scott had a string of cheese on his chin and his mouth open for a chomp of pizza when Dad ordered, "Hold it, Scott. I want to propose a toast in McSwiggen well water." He raised a jelly glass. "To my younger son, Mark, who showed a lot of gumption. More than I thought he had."

Mark was sure no picnic of the coming summer could beat the first one of the season. He trailed after Kelli, who pointed out garden flowers pushing up around the schoolhouse. She was glad Mrs. McSwiggen would be there to see them all bloom. With her back next door, Kelli was sure she would finish her final review and pass the test.

"And she's not even a teacher," Mark observed.

"She doesn't teach exactly. She just makes sure you learn." Kelli noticed a cluster of little dark red sprouts a few inches above the ground. "Those peonies are my favorites. If you hadn't used your bean, they'd be under the asphalt. Also, Mark, if you hadn't given me the GED study guide from your garage sale, I'd still be sneezing as I worked at Charley's Chicken."

Kelli's green eyes were clear and sparkling as the sun on a grass blade.

"Your allergies! They're a whole lot better."

"Gone," Kelli stated. "Today the doctor finally pinned it down. It was the coating on Charley's Chicken. My job was to roll the pieces in that mixture."

"What's in it?"

"Who knows?" Kelli shrugged. "That coating, whatever it has in it, is not good for me. I'm glad you helped me get away from it."

Mark felt proud of himself. "Do you think I'll be Academically Talented, AT, same as you?"

Kelli brushed his hair down. "It wouldn't surprise me."

When the mail jeep passed, Kelli went off to check the Fryes' box. Dad dozed on Mrs. McSwiggen's step. Mom, with her head on his shoulder, took a nap, too. In a sunny spot away from the building Scott lay facedown on the grass.

Mark walked his fingers up Scott's spine. "Well-developing musculature."

Scott sat up and put on his cap. "Yeah, Mark, *we* did all right, and I do mean *we:* Mrs. McSwiggen for rolling the weights into our place; you for working out with me. Lifting did it. Dr. Feluchi took time to talk to me. He says to keep up the good work."

"Scott, it really is *we*. The weights worked for me, too. I took care of the Skinners. They won't mess with Mark Frye. They'll need something else for amusement."

Scott listened closely as Mark described the encounter complete with demonstration swings. He felt Mark's upper arm. "One thing's sure. It wasn't muscle. You must have done it with concentration and adrenaline."

"What's adrenaline?"

"Your brain gets a signal to shoot this stuff from a gland when you're mad or in danger. Makes you extra strong."

"Did Dr. Feluchi tell you about it?"

"He didn't need to. We had that in school. He did tell me that lifting strengthened my back muscles, but not yours. The truth is you don't yet have enough muscle tone to develop. You won't have until you're about my age."

Mark struck a boxer's stance. "Well, as long as I have this adrenaline and I concentrate."

Kelli came with the mail. "Here's a letter for Mom from Kroger's. An ad, I guess."

Mom roused up and took her letter. She rubbed her eyes as if to make sure she was awake. "I'm flabbergasted. This is from Kroger's, but it's no ad. The deli manager read in the *Herald* that I won first prize at the International. Look at this." She handed the letter to Dad. "She wants to know if I'll decorate their special-order cakes. Their decorator is moving in a month to the Sunbelt. It's part-time work. Just what I want. Imagine. If I take the job, I'll get paid for something I like to do."

They all urged Mom to take the job and promised to be extra helpful at home. Mom said she knew she could put Mark in charge of desserts.

Kelli sorted through the rest of the mail. "Here's a beautiful picture of Grand Canyon." She turned the card over. "It's for Mark. Mrs. McSwiggen got there all right."

"Let me have it." Mark snatched the card and read: "Dear Mark, I rode to the bottom on a mule. Pretty sore the next day—ha-ha. I got 19 mpg from the old wagon coming out. I'm heading back to Hardin Grove now. Figure out what to do. Take care of everything for me. Love from Grand Canyon and your friend, Edna F. McSwiggen."

Mark felt he had indeed taken care of things quite well.

* * *

Mrs. McSwiggen returned a few days later. Mom forbade Mark to bother her while she was busy with lawyers, Max Bookout, the mall company, the locksmith, carpenters, and a sign painter.

When he finally had a chance to have a proper visit with her, he was amazed to find the schoolhouse more crowded than ever. Mrs. McSwiggen wore blue jeans and a Grand Canyon T-shirt. She'd said Mark wouldn't see her wig again. She'd forgotten it in an Indiana motel and hadn't bothered to go back for it. She explained to Mark that Tag Mickelson had helped her out with stock. He needed good display space, and she'd have it right next to the mall. She could also help him with values.

Mark moved crocks from a bench so he could sit. "Mom sure is happy about her desk. She just knows her great-great-grandfather worked on that very one. It's exactly like the one she had except it doesn't need refinishing."

Mrs. McSwiggen nodded. "I could tell she was tickled pink. Tag Mickelson is almost as good a spotter as I am. He saw it coming up at auction out on Route Forty-eight." She nudged Mark. "To tell you the truth, Tag gave me a real good price on that desk. He was grateful to have Izannah Walker back and to know her true value. You will have that desk someday, Mark. It's really a gift to you, too."

"I never had such an expensive present before."

Mrs. McSwiggen sat down on an old quilt beside him.

"It was the least I could do, considering you saved my home and future business."

"Are you sure? How about that flaw in your title?"

Mrs. McSwiggen spread her hands. "Mended. Good as new. When your folks showed my lawyer that old paper signed by M. L. Hardin, he got a payday move on and appealed to the county judge to issue an order keeping the mall company off my property until my whole case could be reviewed in light of the new evidence."

Mrs. McSwiggen went on to explain that the judge was honest as the day is long and that her case was most unusual. In the end the mall company had to give up claim to her land.

"Wasn't it strange that M. L. Hardin's paper was right next door the whole time?" Mark asked.

Mrs. McSwiggen agreed. She thought it was a wonder the mice hadn't got to it and chewed it up or that it hadn't turned up long ago. More than thirty years had gone by since Max Bookout was director and clerk of Hardin Creek School. He always was careless. She thought he took after the first clerk of the district, back in 1848, who didn't secure a land deed.

"Max kept all the school records in that desk," Mrs. McSwiggen said. "One slips out and sticks behind a drawer. Nothing to him. Before Max went from school director to politics, the Bookouts all worked for the Hardins. They lived between here and the creek. No doubt about it, your mother's folks bought the desk when the Bookout place was cleared out. It's fallen down now."

Mark thought of the old foundation stones in the Outback. "Their lilac bush is still there."

Mrs. McSwiggen got up and moved an old milk can. "Retail business is very confining, Mark. Tag will help, but both of us will need time off to take in Saturday garage sales and auctions. Would you like to give us a hand then for a few hours?"

The answer was on the tip of Mark's tongue, but he hesitated. Mrs. McSwiggen stirred up a fog of dust with her broom. "You're good at meeting the public. You think about that job."

Mark did as he detoured home through the Outback. He was sure he didn't want to spend a single hour of a single Saturday among a clutter of crocks, china, and curios. Even if the job paid well, being rich wasn't enough. He had other things to do.

Still, he didn't want to be ungrateful to Mrs. McSwiggen and refuse her offer. He'd help until he'd worked out the cost of the weights. Then maybe he'd just forget to show up anymore for work.

A few weeks later Mark went to help get ready for the grand opening of Schoolhouse Antiques. An eye-catching sign was in place outside. Inside, a clipping from the *Herald* was posted by the boys' cloakroom entrance. Mark had memorized the headline: LANDMARK SCHOOL-HOUSE SAVED FROM BULLDOZER. ALERT YOUTH FINDS

CRUCIAL RECORD. One picture showed Mark, Dirty Belly, the police, and Izannah Walker with the bulldozer in the background. The second photo, which Mrs. McSwiggen gave the *Herald*, had been taken some fifteen years earlier. The smaller headline read: HARDIN ROAD RESIDENT TO OPEN SCHOOLHOUSE ANTIQUES.

Mrs. McSwiggen put Mark right to work. "See what's in this box. It came from Tag, and it's hard telling what he's dragged in. You might come across some country primitives. That's the latest."

Mark pulled out a heavy kraut cutter, discarded a broken basket, set aside a book.

Mrs. McSwiggen put a bouquet of lilacs on a windowsill. "We're more than square on the weight lifting set. Now we have a clean slate. I'll need you the next two Saturdays. Big auctions coming up."

Mark said okay but felt miserable. He really wanted to tell her he wouldn't come, but he didn't know how to start. He could hear Kelli saying, "You don't tell anybody. You just do things."

Near the bottom of the carton he came to a mask, not a Halloween mask but an odd one made of braided corn husks. The Zanzutus could have made it and could teach him to braid masks. He, in turn, could not in his entire life even describe to them all the world's wonders.

The job was too big. He alone couldn't bring the Zanzutus up-to-date. Mark would resign his impossible position as chief engineer, supreme judge, and school superintendent of the Zanzutus. He'd leave the Zanzutus and work at things he could handle. They could manage without him.

Although he'd left the Zanzutus behind, he was grateful to them. Without saying a word, they had shown him how much he had to learn. Like Kelli's old toys, they had served their purpose. Before he could teach anyone, Mark needed to know a lot more himself—especially about values. He'd make a start.

Mark showed Mrs. McSwiggen the mask and suggested she give it to the Hardin Grove Historical Society. Then he stood watching her rearrange a display of cut glass.

"What is it, Mark?" she asked. "Something on your mind?"

"Yes. I want to talk to you about something. This spring and summer I'll have an awesome lot to do. I work out with Scott, and we're rebuilding his Honda. I have extra swimming classes at the Y. Grass to mow. Help with housework because Mom and Kelli both have new jobs. Probably I'll go on some runs with Dad to keep him company. I'll read books from the library like this one I found in that box."

"*How Things Work.*" Mrs. McSwiggen read aloud the title of the book he showed her. "You'll learn a lot from that. Just take that along, Mark. Sounds like a good one."

"And I saw a basketball hoop up on the garage of the

house down the road. Some new kids must have moved in. That ought to be fun."

She nodded. "So what are you trying to tell me?"

"That I'll come visit you, but I can't take your job. Don't count on me."

"Well, that's understandable with your schedule. I'm glad you told me."

Mark was relieved and surprised at how simple it was to talk things over. He'd learned something already. It wasn't high technology, but it was important. He felt honest as the day is long.

Mrs. McSwiggen took up her dustcloth. "All right, one last lick. Let's pitch in and finish this job in two shakes of a sheep's tail."

Mark was still full of pep when he left work at School-house Antiques. He ran down the road, feeling free and unburdened. His thoughts went back to what Dad had said about him the day he saved Mrs. McSwiggen's home and business. Dad was right. He, Mark Frye, kid of the late twentieth century, had a lot of gumption. He could do his part.

On his way to check out the new neighbors he stopped and threw a stone at a beer can in the Wilderness Area Swamp. His first pitch pinged the target. For a fellow with muscle development still to come, he sure was in great shape.